ROOT

New stories from North East writers

First published 2013 by IRON Press
5 Marden Terrace
Cullercoats
North Shields
NE30 4PD
tel/fax +44(0)191 2531901
ironpress@blueyonder.co.uk
www.ironpress.co.uk

ISBN 978-0-9565725-5-4

Printed by Fieldprint Ltd
Boldon on Tyne

IRON Press Books are distributed by Central Books
and represented by Inpress Books Ltd
Churchill House, 12 Mosley Street
Newcastle upon Tyne, NE1 1DE
Tel: 44(0) 191 2308104
www.inpressbooks.co.uk

Root

*New stories from
North East writers*

Edited by
Kitty Fitzgerald

CONTENTS

Foreword   7

Jane Roberts-Morpeth   CHARYBDIS   11

Angela Readman   THERE'S A WOMAN WORKS
                       DOWN THE CHIP SHOP   17

Stephen Shieber   BIRDMAN   28

Crista Ermiya   SIGNS OF THE LAST DAYS   35

Rob Walton   CRAZY PAVING   45

Shelley Day Sclater   PICNICKING WITH MY FATHER   59

Eileen Jones   THE HOUSE   67

Avril Joy   TOUGH LOVE   81

John N Price   A BITTER FROST   94

Fiona Cooper   THE GOLDEN VALLEY LINE   102

Judy Walker   SIEVING THE EARTH   114

Beda Higgins   WAITING   124

Amanda Baker   THE REMAINDER   134

Rosemary Brydon   DAFT JOHN   149

Pauline Plummer   GOEBBEL'S HOUSE   162

Biographical Notes   169

FOREWORD

THIS IS THE THIRD ANTHOLOGY OF STORIES I HAVE EDITED FOR *IRON Press*. The first, *IRON Women* (1990) was published when there were three magazines in the region, *IRON Magazine*, *Stand* and *Panurge* that were regularly publishing short stories. However, women were under-represented and Peter Mortimer asked me to edit a collection written by women. Submissions were open to all women. *IRON Women* contained eighteen stories by writers like Helen Dunmore, who had already published three poetry collections, Leland Bardwell, who had published four novels, stories and poetry and others like Anna McGrail and Wendy Wallace who at that time had published nothing.

In 2001, when the second anthology, *Biting Back* was published, there were no longer any print magazines publishing literary fiction left in the region. This time we invited male and female writers who had already been published to submit. There had been an upsurge of successful fiction by writers based here and the anthology showcased newly published writers like Andrea Badenoch and Chrissie Glazebrook, alongside more long standing authors such as David Almond, Julia Darling, Wendy Robertson and Christopher Burns.

This new collection of stories is by writers living in North East England. There was no theme. The stories didn't have to be set in the region or be about it. They didn't have to be new writers, published writers or writers of any particular age or gender. Giving writers free rein to write what they wanted was the thing and the only restriction was the length, 4000 words. The entries were anonymous, with two exceptions.

Firstly, *The Newcastle Journal*, a daily paper, working in association with *New Writing North* recently began publishing stories in their Saturday edition. We liked one of these so much we asked the writer if she would like to submit it for the anthology. Secondly, earlier in the year I had judged the stories in a competition run by North Tyneside Libraries and I asked the winner of that to submit to the anthology.

I read all the stories – there were hundreds – and made an initial shortlist of fifty. Peter Mortimer (IRON Press editor) read this shortlist and then we discussed the stories one by one. Some were immediately earmarked for acceptance and a shorter shortlist was made of those that needed a little editing. We made editing and rewriting suggestions to these writers, an unusual move but one we believed was worthwhile. Eventually fifteen writers were chosen for inclusion. Our commiserations to writers who came tantalisingly close, especially Jeff Price, Annie Macmillan, Helen Graham, C G Allan and Noreen Rees

Three of the stories were written by men and twelve by women. The subject matter ranges through: loss, adoption, gardens, family relationships, death rituals, what God wears, sea mysteries, bullying, a vindictive house, fertility councils and cloning, a woman who morphs into Elvis, tough love, a circus 'bearded lady' and a paparazzi journalist. The writing styles are as different as the subject matter but they all pack a punch. I hope this collection will be a welcome addition to the wonderful literary heritage of the North East.

Kitty Fitzgerald, Cullercoats, 2013

CHARYBDIS

Jane Roberts-Morpeth

GOD WEARS RED CONVERSE ALL STARS WITH RED LACES AND SCUFFED souls, a bit like me. In his pockets he holds string, orange tic-tacs, a tin whistle and a very small, very grumpy cherub called Sid. So says my grandfather, but I confess I'm not wholly convinced. My parents tell me that God resides in Cullercoats Fisherman's Mission Church, caught in frozen piety in the windows that paint my skin with rainbows as I fidget below them on Saint Sunday. He is in the blossoms that fill tall vases by the aisle, but as these blooms are rootless dead shrubbery I'm not sure this is true.

From the church we walk to the clammy warmth of my Grandfather's home, a spit away over the street. I think it's odd; a fisherman's cottage with its back to the sea and the outdoor toilet that my mother finds so awful.

Within there is the swoosh of wind in the chimney dressing my cold fingers with a dream of ice and snow. I hide on the sofa beneath a blanket that holds the ghosts of tobacco and licorice past. A shattering of brick shards ping the grate and the fury outdoors is brought within. If God exists then he must be this force that throws all shades of grey against the old glass panes and weaves a siren song amongst their draughts. My parents mutter of blasphemy at such pronouncements, threaten to stop me from visiting the old man who fills my head with such nonsense.

My mother frets at leaving me here but there is no choice. She needs to be with Broken Hearted Baby in the place that nature left behind. Locked doors, pink walls all coated by a metallic taint; they crowd the plastic box that holds the heart of their new child. I prefer to be here, in a world formed by weather where I can listen from my bed to the hissing of waves on shale.

At the dawn I find God in the snow that has filled the crevices in the back yard until all looks saint dressed in lace finery. He finds kindness in His aluminum clouds beneath which my grandfather and I gaze at a world clothed in wraiths, illuminated only by the stain of the sun as it finds the edge of the sky, staining the metal with fingers of flame.

Down to the harbour. I'm watching smoke emerge from brown pipes chewed over by strong men as they land their catch. A pink eel surges over the side of the basket, his mouth ringed with teeth like the gateway to the plains of hell where the bad dead go. I affect bravery with a finger, then recoil as the cauled eyes quest towards me and I spy the tiny swords ringing its throat.

The men laugh, and Grandfather rumbles in annoyance. A silver flask appears and they pass it round, slurping contentedly. We sit by the Watch House for hours sampling other flasks brim full of bitter coffee. No one seems to remember my mother's plea to remember I'm a child and I'm keen not to remind anyone, even if the brew makes me want to spit. I suck the coffee through my teeth, grounds catching in the cracks. My feet no longer feel the benefit of their boots and I huddle closer into my navy duffel coat as we watch the birds drift on the thermals, singing an eerie song.

Later, after Grandfather remembers to feed me, I watch speckles of light shimmering in the wood in the grate as he brings down the bathtub from the outdoor toilet wall. There's a brass kettle stained with age that he's hung from a hook in the hearth, the water shaking the lid with violent life.

I get first go, and steer my tub through Dark Water Carpet, past the threadbare Needles of Wrath and the Whirlpool of Charybdis that Grandfather tells me is created by a monster.

'Like the eel at the harbour?'

'No boy, a vengeful woman turned into a giant bladder by the Greek gods for theft. Her mouth inhales the sea and spits it back into swirls to catch sailors for dinner.'

'What's a bladder?'

He regards me with slanted eyes that vanish into the crevices in his cheeks when he smiles. 'You know bladderwrack, boy?'

I do, that black-podded seaweed with air pockets that you can pop. He tells me a bladder is like the black poppy pods, magnified a million times.

I don't sleep so well that night. Charybdis is playing on the shale, with the red eel and all of his cousins for arms. Hell at each fingertip.

God remembers the darkness of the void, which he scattered with stars to give himself points of anchor. I think He's a little afraid of shade, which gives us something in common. When the voices wake me I can see Sirius's cold light through the skylight. Stars are prettier than Charybdis, I don't know why they call him the dog.

There are voices below and crying; that hot gulping sound that comes from the throat when the nose can't breathe for water.

Broken Hearted Baby has gone to be with Jesus. They tell me she has a special place where damaged children can be fixed, filled with toys and sunlight, and cookies with orange Smarties. That's why I'm supposed to believe in Him, to book my place there if the unfortunate happens and I'm swallowed by death.

I'm not sure I believe their stories anymore.

We're on the boat, at the prow and I'm shouting defiance to the waves as we surge beyond the harbour walls in a rare umber sunrise. My mother is beside me, grandfather clutching her fist. Father is being sick at the rear; the fishermen pat him on the shoulder when he refuses the silver flask they offer as medicinal.

I can see the horizon curving, the sky melting into the sea and I wonder whether it will be Charybdis or God that takes Broken Hearted Baby when we give her to the water. My mother slaps my grandfather when I ask, and he stares at her with the water in his beard beginning to freeze like her eyes already have.

'I knew this was a stupid idea'. Her voice is like steam rattling a pan lid with temper.

He shrugs hopelessly, and shakes the ice from his beard as Dad staggers to stand by us.

'It's time' he murmurs, touching my mother's cheek gently.

'It'll never be time,' she answers, but softly, like all the steam has gone to drift on the vapour of the waves.

We move to the bow. The priest walks uncertainly, feet roiling on the bleached wood of the deck. He can't grasp the rail like us because he's clutching Broken Hearted Baby. At least that's what I'm told by Dad but I'm wondering how even a small child could fit into such a tiny jar. It is pretty I think, with blue sky and green fields oddly bright on this steel sea.

There's a scattering in the air, drifts of gray grit that falls to the sea over a song of loss. I'm standing eyes wide, as a second arc is flung by my mother, then yet more by her father and then mine, faces pale as Grandfather's condensed milk.

'Gone to God,' my mother murmurs, her fingers catching my hair briefly.

The jar must be empty; they turn and head for the relative shelter of the prow and I am forgotten as my skin sticks to the rail and wind fingers poke my spine.

The sun breaks for a moment, settling on the surf where the ash has fallen. The water churns in our wake and fear fills my mouth with bitter liquid. *She* is coming for my sister, I know this and I cannot help her, I can only watch as her hands exit the water first, their sea serpent heads questing the air blindly. As She unfurls her body my knees fail and I watch from between the rails, bottom lip cut as I fell. Her eyes meet mine, such aquamarine eyes beneath a crown of pearls. Charybdis regards me gravely as the waters gather pace about her. My blood spatters the sea thinly and she nods, just once, and I realize that she is beautiful.

More beautiful than God in his rainbow window.

The eels gather below the surface. Cupped within their centre a smaller vortex forms, drawing together a simmering mass of ash. Charybdis pulls it against her breast and form emerges, a scarcely seen creature that is still as familiar as my own hands. Different now, silvered like a glint of sun on the waves.

The sun flickers and vanishes. I blink, and she has gone.

There's a Woman Works Down the Chip Shop

Angela Readman

My mother was like a Custard Cream, nothing special, an ordinary sort of nice enough. She was just there, like gravity, or the white dog mess that appeared outside the bookies on Mondays. There was no need to think about her. She was Mam-shaped, bits of her slightly flattened under a white overall with pearly buttons. Then, one summer, she became Elvis. She yawned, frying chips, and worrying if there'd be enough hot water for a bath when she got in, then BAM! She was Elvis, hips jiggling, rocking onto the balls of her feet with only the counter between her and lasses screaming and promising to love her forever. Maybe she just thought, 'Sod it. I'd make as good an Elvis as anyone.' Who doesn't want to be Elvis now and then?

The funny thing is, I don't think my mother was *ever* an Elvis girl. The stereogram went on only on Sunday mornings. She dusted with the aid of Julie Andrews singing about hills and a nun's favourite things. All her Beatles records were before Lucy in the Sky. I sat on the carpet and flipped through my mother's singles, her name written on in a tight scroll round the run-out groove. I suppose she must have went places she might lose them, but I couldn't see where. She left school, got a job at the dogs and married the bloke who set the rabbit running. *If* she was *ever* going to be Elvis, you'd think it would be then – somewhere between school and the man who made a greyhound whip itself into the shape of a winner. No. For my mother, being Elvis took time. We never deliberately listened to the King, but knew how to dance to him. Maybe that's what she needed, someone who *just knew* the words to her songs.

Everyone knew my mother from the waist up. She was the woman in the chippy – a portion on the stingy side for spitters and folks with tattoos, overly generous to anyone who said 'Please' and 'Thank you' (never 'Ta'.) She knew if her regulars were the mushy peas or beans sort. That's all. Then, came that lass. The lass looked like someone who got into her Mam's make-up box and went mad. Black stuff all over on her eyelids like tyre-tracks, her gaze was the victim of a crash. Chips. A mist of salt. No vinegar. Red cola. She came in with a slobbery ginger bairn in a pram and a fistful of coins like a piggy bank spewed in her hand.

'You want scraps?'

Mam held the vinegar, snowed on the salt and turned to the fridge for pop.

'I like your bobble,' the lass said.

'Sorry?'

She said it again.

Mam's hair came home every night smelling of other people's suppers. It grew long and dark and waiting for her to decide to be a beatnik to make it feel at home. It was permanently scraped back with one of my bobbles. This one had white spots on red like a dice. What are the chances anyone would notice something so small? Who cares? Mam looked sort of stunned. Who comments on a bobble? There was something sad or lovely about it, it was hard to tell. The lass lined up coins on the steel in order of size. Nice enough lass. Friendly. Why? Mam double wrapped the chips and threw in a free sachet of ketchup to hide her embarrassment.

On Saturday she came in with a haircut short enough to stop her needing to hold anything back. I ran my fingers along tapered hair, the back of my mother's head felt like suede. No accessories needed. No comment required. She didn't do much with it, but every morning, without trying, the top of her head rose in a quiff, a wave swallowing her ordinariness.

'What's with this hair?' she murmured, 'got a mind of its own.'

She patted it down; it popped back up.

'You look like my woodwork teacher, thinks he's all that,' Brian said.

I noticed just how black my mother's hair really was. It was the sort of black that made me look at roads and crows and decide 'black' needed more names. Elvis was waiting to enter the building. I don't think she could have stopped it if she tried.

She couldn't stop the lass with the ginger kid fancying chips.

'Long day, rushed off your feet I bet? Not long now,' the lass said, looking at the clock on the wall.

My mother lowered the basket into hissing fat and paused to look at the lass. Eczema on her knuckles, inquisitive chin.

Her mouth had a look about it like it wanted to smile, if the woman behind the counter said anything that let it. I suppose my mother wasn't used to considering how long she'd worked or if her feet hurt. They just existed, in a perpetual state of half-ache. She fastened her eyes on the lass now and unexpectedly smiled. A curl softly tugged her top lip. It wasn't her usual smile. It was all Elvis, a smile that lets a second breathe. I noticed her mouth was the same shape as Elvis, how she looked just like him in the face. I never thought: if Elvis was a lass, and worked in a chippy, he'd be my mam. And now, I could hardly see her for Elvis. Elvis jiggled the chips, hips tick tocking like an over wound clock, all because someone asked how she was. It was like the difference between being Elvis and not being Elvis was as simple as someone *really* looking and wondering how you feel.

'You're my last customer,' Mam said, like it was special.

When Elvis said it, it was.

Then, as if forgetting something, she added, 'Cute bag.'

The bag was a stringy thing full of holes. Impractical, my mother would have called it, if she'd noticed. But Elvis liked it. The lass wriggled her fingers in and out of her bag's strings, little fish caught in a net. Elvis grinned.

'Have fun,' the lass said, hugging her chips.

The woman behind the counter watched her walk out past the manager pulling down the shutters. She smiled, leaning back against the yellow glass windows of the lamp heating the pies. Elvis stretched like a cat in the sun. 'Have fun?' she drawled. It was an order no one ever placed. Elvis tugged a pouty lip, considering what it meant.

Now, I don't know exactly how often the lass came in the chippy, or when Gina became her name. I only got scraps, bits after and what I saw when I called in for pop or change for Spangles. I do know, there was nothing special about Gina, except how she talked. Gina made conversation like a gardener, planting a seed and waiting to see what might grow. None of us knew a woman like that. Women in Hinton's were snipers. 'How you keeping?' was a loaded gun, mouths cocked, aimed to shoot rounds; Mam turned her trolley around to avoid friendly fire.

What really did it is wiring. Gina came in with a lamp bigger than her. Mam's quiff stood to attention. Behind the counter, the bottom half of her body tilted in a different direction all on its own.

'Youboughtsomethingnicesugar?' she said.

Now, this wasn't my mother at all. She was all salt 'n' vinegar, the odd splash of ketchup, but the way she spoke now made the lass shiver like velvet had been draped along her neck.

'Lamp for the living room, if I ever get the plug on,' Gina said.

The woman in the chippy would have sympathised, but it wasn't her job to do more. Elvis had other ideas. He offered to take care of business. Mam went to Gina's after work with a screwdriver in her pocket. She wired the lamp, somehow turning her Elvisness on full-time.

Everything was different. It was the summer of Elvis, and Mam having a friend she didn't give to birth to. Gina lived on the estate where houses had gardens. We stopped

21

sunbathing in our slice of yard where sun hid behind the walls. The ginger toddler, Simon, bounced up and down in Gina's open back door. We sat in the garden, the grown-ups pulling weeds and mowing wonky lines in the lawn. They did all the usual stuff, but somehow it wasn't boring. Elvis made it a breeze. Carrying stuff out for the scrap-man, the adults held one side of a fridge apiece, then creased up laughing like it told a joke. Elvis' laugh made my mother's old one sound like something running out of batteries, barely used. The sun blazed and she shone, her skin a gold suit. She washed windows with a hose and turned it on Gina. Gina ducked and dived about the garden, laughing, soaked. The wifey next door put out her rubbish and lingered by the fence on tip toes, slippers getting streaked with grass. She stood there a long time, unable to tear her eyes off Elvis making the woman next door laugh.

'You making that sarnie or what?' her husband yelled through the back door.

I watched the smile on her face twitch like a curtain. She went in, looking back.

I sat on top of the coal bunker, the felt almost burning my legs. Brian tossed stones.

'Why do we have to come here?' he said, 'What's Mam doing that stupid smile for all the time?'

I looked down at Elvis and Gina taking a break; two tatty towels lay side by side on the grass. Their eyes closed then opened. They turned towards each other and spoke so quietly only a bee flying over might hear. Brian's ears were red with listening. Brothers. He didn't like being at Gina's. He liked it even less when her water heater broke and she stayed at ours. Even when we went to Sandsend for the day, he walked ahead on his own, cheeks red as a slapped bum.

Elvis took Gina's hand to walk across the unsteady dunes. Then dropped it like it burnt. Someone was coming, an old man and a woman let a ratty dog do its business. I looked at the old woman from my Nan's street. What was her name? Gwenny; everyone my Nan knew was a Gwenny or something like it. Every morning the women crossed paths on the way to the newsagents, stopping to chat, flowery headscarves flapping like parrots in the wind.

'What's wrong?' Gina said.

She looked at my mother, looking down as if she'd lost something in the sand. The old man shook his head. The old woman said something I wasn't sure I heard. I think it was, 'You should be ashamed.'

Not till they were out of sight, and Gina had set up a windbreaker fort on the beach, did I see Elvis again. Somewhere along the path my mother took his place.

Then she was gone again – buried. Elvis grinned at his body of sand, the mermaid tail weighting his hips. I swear, no one could stop looking. This was Elvis, right here. Elvis – suddenly bursting out of the shell of his sand tail and picking up Gina to toss in the sea like she weighed less than the shopping bags Mam usually balanced like the scales of justice.

'Do you like Gina, honey?' Elvis asked, tucking me in, sleepy with sea.

'I wished we lived with her all the time,' I said.

Mam sighed like an Elvis who didn't want to be famous, an Elvis realising the guitar he clutched was too small.

The queue in the chip shop didn't move as fast as it used to. Sometimes lasses hovered at the counter. Smiling at Elvis, they looked up at the menu unable to decide what they wanted. An Elvis pelvis rocked to the sizzle of fat like music. He whirled chips into paper and span around, laying them down. Some girls applauded and blushed, placing their hands over their mouths to stop their hearts leaping out. And some didn't. They folded their arms. The lady who lived next door to Gina twisted her hands as her husband tapped fingers on his wallet.

'What the fuck's taking so long?' he said.

Elvis turned from the pie window, walked slowly to the counter and leaned forward.

'That's no way to talk in front of a lady, Sir,' he said, head bowed.

'Pardon?' the man said. He looked at the queue of old men behind him, blokes back from the football, and his wife beside him. 'I'll talk how the fuck I like in front of her, she's my wife,' he said.

'Maybe you should apologise,' Elvis said.

The wife tugged her husband's arm, 'Leave it,' she said.

He shrugged off her hand and pushed her into a stagger. Elvis shook his head slowly, then WHAM! A fist landed square on the man's jaw with a cowboy loud crack. Kids pressed their noses to the window, trying to get a good look in, 'Fight, fight, fight, fight...' The man hit the deck, the queue twittered and scattered around him like sparrows.

'You'll be sorry,' he said, hand on his jaw.

'I am sorry,' Elvis said, 'I'm sorry for your wife.'

Everyone talked about the fight for weeks. The woman in the fishy went mental and knocked a guy out for no reason, people said. No, she gave him a black eye for pushing in the queue. No one was sure, not even the manager who was at his sister's wedding. No one actually complained. Elvis apologised to everyone who was there. It was free chips, no, it was free fishcakes, all round.

It wasn't the punch that changed things, I don't think, it was something quieter that finally wiped the Elvis off my mother's face. It was pension night. The Gwenny who lived near my Nan popped in for supper on her way back from bingo.

'What can I get you?' Elvis beamed.

The old woman's mouth was a zip, syllables caught in her teeth.

'*You* can't get me anything,' she said.

The queue shuffled and whispered. They looked at Elvis, then at the glaring woman and whispered again.

The old woman didn't place her order, and she didn't budge.

'What can I do for you?' the manager said.

He smoothed his comb-over over and walked to the counter to dip her haddock in the batter himself.

I looked towards Elvis, coins for Pineappleade sweating in my hand. Elvis wasn't there, just my mother, filling the box of wooden forks, looking like someone booed offstage.

'You still hanging about with that lass? What's her face?' Nan said; her lips were a line.

'No.'

Nan nodded, broke out her stash of Bullseyes and squirreled them back in her bag.

'Hear her husband's back. Shame you can't find a good solid man,' Nan said.

'You make blokes sound like tower-blocks,' Mam said.

She looked out the window as if imagining women who lived within the walls of good solid men – constantly moving the furniture, re-painting the doors.

Elvis had left the building. He wasn't in the chippy or at home. Mam brought in tea and biscuits, putting the tin down like it weighed a tonne. I picked a biscuit out the tin and looked at the Custard Cream, the scrolly pattern like an invitation on old fashioned note paper, then I dunked it in my tea. Mam hunched over the newspaper looking at ads for people next to lost cats and dogs. She circled 'GSOH' with a pen. A week later, stepping out of the house in heels she was Bambi learning ice.

'Did you have a nice time?' I said.

She took two bags of crisps out her bag and tossed us one each.

Brian buried his face in Commando.

'It was OK.'

I licked prawn cocktail off my crisps.

'Is no one nice?'

'They are, but… I dunno, there's just…no…no… chemistry,' she said, slumping onto the couch.

It didn't seem like she was talking to me or Brian exactly. It was more something she had to say to herself, like the way she figured out the crossword by saying words aloud and counting the letters on her fingers. I listened, picturing men in test tubes. My mother's laugh was a scientist, none of her experiments succeeded in reviving Elvis. She put her heels back in the box and wrapped fish suppers in ads for men who liked long walks. Elvis was AWOL.

I didn't see so much as a trace of him until tatty picking week the following year, when some woman started popping into the chip shop on her way back from work.

'You always put on just the right splash of vinegar,' she said.

She clutched a note, looking at my mother. She leaned up to the counter with a grin, sandals slipping off the backs of her feet. Chips. Pineapple ring. Curry Sauce.

'Quiet night, eh?' she said.

And there was Elvis again, for a heartbeat, as if he never left and was just waiting in the wings – if my mother would allow him to make a comeback. Elvis looked at the lass – tufty brown hair, pianist fingers laid flat on the counter, no rings, dimples between her eyes and lips. The woman in the chippy shook off a smile and stormed on the salt.

'You want scraps?' she said.

Birdman

Stephen Shieber

EACH DAY, SINCE THE LAST DAY OF FEBRUARY, I MAKE MY LITTLE pilgrimage up to the bridge, still hiding behind funeral black. Each day my fingers worry the packet of stale bread in my pocket until it turns to mush and is no longer fit for the ducks. Each day, I sit on the bench longer and longer, waiting for something to arrive. When it comes, I'll know it and, until it does, I stay, hoping to save a life, any life, knowing that I can't save mine.

I notice him the day spring slides quietly into summer. He's hiding too, behind the urban uniform of hoodie and joggers. As soon as he sees me, he turns away, making my heart contract as he lays his head on the parapet, splaying his bony fingers between the painted rivet-heads. I almost weep at the inhuman sigh that carries the weight of his suffering.

I won't let him become the tenth jumper of the year, the tenth lost husband, or brother, or son. I won't let his picture find a place in that newspaper gallery of nine, mostly overdrawn bankers and estateless agents. Whatever good he's done isn't going to shrivel up and die in the glaring heat of one fatal lack of judgment.

The Samaritans have done well with their posters, but they can't be as effective as an on-site presence, especially one with my experience.

I'll add this man to my tally of the Saved. Since February, I've developed a series of strategies for saving potentials from going over the top. I've encouraged the hopeless, heckled the resolute and feigned madness to confuse the undecided. What does it matter if they see me as a crazy-haired, middle-aged woman with a houseful of cats? Life is worth infinitely more than reputation.

Wiping worried hands on my coat, I reach out to him and touch his shoulder. His raspberry eyes blaze with suspicion. I do my best to disguise my disgust with sympathy. I'm no expert, but his skin complaint is way beyond acne. His face is grey and his features small and sharp, dwarfed by the milky carbuncle lying along his brow.

My scrutiny is unwelcome. He shakes it off by extending his scalloped neck, mottled with emerald bruises, as if someone's taken great pains to throttle him for art's sake. I try to smile encouragingly, but my facial muscles are rusty, producing instead an unwelcoming grimace.

The hood slips back from my new friend's small, domed skull and I catch a mouthful of the scent of rubbish baking in overflowing bins, making me choke and my eyes water. If I stay downwind of him I'll be ok. And I have to honour my promise, the only thing I can treasure now that my wedding vows are null and void.

When I can speak, I ask him, 'Are things really this bad?' I know the answer already, because it lies like an iron bar over my heart.

He looks at me again, triangular mouth open, pointed tongue struggling to curl round vowels and consonants. Through his trilling, I detect a single word.

'North. North.'

We're as far north as I'd ever wanted to be, here because of Brian's work, the work that drove him to a similar edge on the other side of the city.

My new friend tilts his head and emits a soft cry that keens through me. I offer him my arm and his whole body shudders at human contact. I wonder what he thinks of himself, of how low he thinks things have sunk to consider such a desperate act on such a beautiful day.

'Who's north? Do you have family there? Do you want to get back to them?'

He makes no effort to answer my questions, opening his mouth only to insist on north repeatedly, until the word becomes music.

Gripping his arm, I hurry him along to the end of the bridge and we take the narrow path down into the park. I feel better on the flat. He can't hope to launch himself from here without failing.

My confidence shrinks, however, when a sudden gust of air whips round us. My agitated friend rises on tiptoe, extending his neck and opening his raw mouth to taste the air. I watch this intimate act with a blush. He tastes the air like a familiar lover.

'Must...go...north.'

He pulls on my arm, restless, looking for approval for his plan. I smile, driven on by a single thought. Keep him away from the bridge, from the object of his obsession, and I can save him.

As we walk through the park, revising students half-heartedly ignore us. Mothers draw their children's prams closer. Kind-hearted souls nod to us and mumble embarrassed greetings, pitying my deformed son. I laugh to myself, wondering what their reaction to the truth might be.

Truth? They've been working these past few months to establish the truth in regards to my husband. What a waste of time and money. The truth is transparent. He blew it and then he flew, leaving me in debt up to my sad little hazel eyeballs.

My new friend has a sixth sense for sympathy. Whenever I think of Brian's suicide, the Birdman wraps his wing around me. Images flood my head, until I suffer vertigo.

As we wander through the petting zoo and pause by the ignorant goats, he offers me a vision so bright and clear that it's like watching one of those roller-coaster films.

I see the bridge and the sad woman in her mourning coat, imprinting her fingers onto the stale bread that she keeps in her pocket. A magnificent being approaches, no longer caught between man and bird, but free to soar above the earth and to enjoy all things in their true perspective.

He beckons to her and she unties the buttons of her coat, letting it pool like tar on the concrete below. I see her glassy toenails as she grips the edge of the bridge before letting go, dropping down, down, until she catches the upward thrust and ascends, thermals roaring through her consciousness. The human world shrinks away and the tree canopy opens to allow her the freedom of the cloud-bearded sky.

One of the ignorant goats bleats me out of my vision and I wait in silence for my companion to verify all I've seen. He bobs his head in confirmation.

'How?'

Now more bird than human, I detect the ghost of his grin. He struts forward, out of my grasp, twisting his head to indicate I should follow. My heart expands at the prospect of escape. I can follow him anywhere. Anywhere, but be left here.

We pass some bins and the Birdman samples their odour with delight. I force him on, still held back by human concerns, to the cafe beyond the waterfall, forgetting our path will lead us past the birdhouse.

The pain of captivity rattles his rib cage and his cry echoes not only in me but in the inhabitants within. The Birdman pecks and scratches the glass cage, inciting a riot.

I try to pull him away, but white-hot anger radiates from him. He puffs up his breast until his feather armour erupts from his human clothes. Desperate to move on, I reach into my pocket and break the corner of a slice of bread as an offering to him. He cocks his head like it's an insult.

The keeper sees us off, a round little man with a wiry moustache and battered cap of authority. He takes one look at the Birdman and addresses me instead.

'Move along, won't you? You're upsetting the birds.'

I shrug. 'Perhaps they don't like to be kept in cages.'

His face twists with displeasure. 'Not one of them Animal Rights people is you? Humans come first in my book and always will.'

I open my mouth to list the startling successes of human beings, but stop when I see that my Birdman has no time for debate. I can't risk him returning to the bridge without me. I don't have room for any more loss.

Catching up with him, I persuade the Birdman to perch at a picnic table while I fetch water and seed-cake. Setting it in front of him, he tears a piece off for me. We have a great distance to fly and both need the sustenance.

The great change starts after just a few mouthfuls. My skin softens and itches as thousands of tiny hillocks march across my limbs. Next is the pain of needles pricking my body from inside. The Birdman sends me flashes of reassurance as I watch my transformation with horrified delight. Feathers burrow through my skin and unfurl like ferns over my lighter, hollow bones.

I try to express my delight and fear, but the words clog in the back of my throat until they sweeten into pure sound. Now I'm ravenous. I lower my head and peck at the sweet, sticky dough until it's all gone. From behind me comes a murmur of human disapproval but, even if I wanted to stop I can't.

From this point, things progress rapidly, according to the pattern of my vision. We race back to the bridge and I have my first taste of flight, hovering inches above the ground. I throw back my head to sing my astonishment, but the Birdman indicates there's no time for displays of wonder. We're ready to leave the heavy earth behind, to float on the air.

I count twelve people on the bridge, all watching our

spectacle unfold. Some people reach for their phones and film us, assuming we're acrobats promoting an exotic circus.

I think of Brian for the last time as the Birdman and I stand claw-to-claw on the parapet. Now I can understand his – their – temptation, all nine of the men featured in the paper. The world looks so beautiful from up here. Not at all frightening or endless or unbearable. Perhaps they, too, thought the answer to their problems was flying.

Some of the spectators scream as the Birdman falls away from the bridge. My avian heart gives a little leap as I watch him. It takes an eternity before he rises again, an arrow aimed at the centre of the sky, his final look for me alone, daring me to follow.

SIGNS OF THE LAST DAYS

Crista Ermiya

SUMMER BEGAN EARLY THAT YEAR; THE AIR GREW HOT AND DUSTY. The city was all haze; cars drove through the heat like water, wavering and flickering right in front of us until we grew afraid to cross the street. Old women wore tight polyester dresses in bright floral prints, sleeveless, squeezed into the breathless fabric like sausage meat, their loose upper arms hanging out liver-spotted and fleshy. Young children cried and grew fractious. Weeds that normally flourished in the cracks of paving stones and broken walls withered and died. The city baked and cracked. The grass in our local park turned brown.

That summer, the radio played the same songs over and over – *Every breath you take, Cruel Summer, Who's that girl?* – until we could no longer tell the difference between the song lyrics and breathing. We skipped school and took the bus to the local High Street, where we stole shell-shaped hairclips from Woolworths, and walked into Marks & Spencers in our old shoes and walked straight out again with bright shiny new pairs in black patent plastic, or white courts with three inch heels that got caught in the grooves on the steps of the bus home.

Once, Miri came with us.

Miri wore flat lace-up shoes, like a man's, and knee-length socks. She was the only girl who wore her school blazer after the first week. When it was cold, she wore a white polo-neck under her shirt. When it was hot, she dispensed with the polo-neck and unbuttoned her collar, but still wore her blazer and the knee-length socks. Some of us knew Miri from primary school, and whispered to the rest that she was strict Seventh Day Adventist. On Saturdays she would go to church with her mother and two baby brothers. She wasn't allowed to eat bacon, or bacon-flavoured crisps, on Saturday or any other day.

Wednesday mornings was Swimming, when we would board a coach to the pools. We knew a girl had started bleeding if she only went swimming three Wednesdays out of every four. But Miri never went swimming at all. We couldn't imagine her in a swimming costume, revealing her legs, her arms. Some reckoned it was the swimming cap that was the problem: her hair was always so carefully pressed.

That Wednesday it was too hot, the air so heavy we couldn't breathe. We skipped the coach, walked out of the school gates, and just carried on walking. It wasn't until we were near the High Street that we realised Miri was with us. She was trailing behind, beads of sweat standing out on her forehead beneath her hairline.

'Miri, you's a bad girl now?'

She managed an uncomfortable smile and looked down at her laced-up feet.

'Take off your blazer,' we commanded.

She shook her head, so we pulled it off her, arms pulled

back behind her torso. But it was too hot for messing, so we dropped it on the side of the road, where she bent down to pick it up. She folded the blazer neatly into her bag and carried on walking after us.

We walked until we reached the entrance to an old cemetery. The gates were wide open and inside we could see a dusty path leading into green shade. We saw the tops of trees move gently in a breeze – a *real* breeze, not hot air blowing into our faces from the rushing traffic out of exhaust pipes. We walked through the gates.

The graves were old and overgrown except near the path, where a row of low rectangular mounds were covered in fragments of glass stone: blue, white, red. We thought, at first, that they were jewels.

'Don't be stupid,' we said, when we realised they weren't. But they were pretty. We picked up handfuls and let them fall through our fingers.

'Stop it,' said Miri. She was a tiny fly on a hot day, not worth the effort of swatting. We picked up more handfuls and poured them into our pockets, into our bags.

'You're stealing from the dead,' said Miri.

'They won't miss them,' we said. 'Relax, girl.'

A white woman in a filthy denim jacket rose up out of the dense foliage smothering the older headstones. A cigarette dangled from her thin fingers and her hair, matted into dreads, was the colour of harvest smoke.

Miri screamed but it came out like a hiccup. The woman staggered towards us.

'Did'nae mean t' startle youse,' she slurred, a can clutched in her other hand. 'Ah'm just visiting my old nan, god rest her soul.'

We didn't say anything.

'Got a light?' she asked.

We lit the cigarette for her. It took a few goes, because she kept swaying out of reach, and once, it fell out of her mouth onto the ground. When the flame took she raised her cigarette hand into a limp thumbs-up sign. Her creased skin edged up around her mouth.

'Cheers. You're sweethearts, all of youse.'

And she disappeared down the path. We burst out laughing, and passed each other our own cigarettes, swiped from mothers and boyfriends, or bought in singles from the sweet-shop across the road from school.

'You want one?' we asked Miri.

She shook her head. We envied her refusal; it was too hot to smoke.

We walked deeper into the cemetery, where it was cooler. The trees were wide and expansive, their growth barely controlled, and we could hardly see the sky for leaves. Around us, headstones became more ornate, in the shape of crosses, angels, or open bibles. We came to a large marble memorial laid down on the ground, inscribed with the names of war dead, and we lay down on top of it, skirts rolled up, arms and legs spread open like starfish on the cool surface.

'And there will be wars, and rumours of wars.'

'What?'

We raised our heads. Miri was standing a few feet away.

'Nothing,' she said.

We read the names of the dead: Adams, D; Athill, D; Atkins, T; rolling down all the way through the alphabet until we got to Young, A.G; Young, C; Young, T. And an inscription: *Non Sibi Sed Patriae.*

'What's that mean?'

'Who cares? They're dead, don't need old-time words to tell us that.'

Miri said, 'Words is how the world was made.'

'Oh shut up girl,' we groaned.

A vein on Miri's left temple pulsed in the heat. The spots on her forehead stood out.

'Miri,' we asked, 'you ever thought about concealer?'

'Yeah, you wear make-up Miri?'

This was met with a slow, silent shake of her head.

'Let's get a little gloss on those chappy lips of yours.'

We weren't bad. We wanted to be kind. Bags were delved into and cosmetics purses retrieved.

'This one, Miri. The colour will suit you.'

She reached out and took the proffered tube of lipstick, eased off the lid, twisted the end, and marvelled at the scarlet that rose up. We gave her a little hand-mirror, plastic pink-backed, that gleamed roundly in her palm. Her hand tilted towards her face, and a circular spot of sunlight danced over a tree behind her. We couldn't see her face reflected: in the angles visible to us were leaves, and gravestones.

Miri stretched her lips into a strange grin and slicked the lipstick over them, in two slow passes that covered her mouth and the surrounding flesh in a pair of rectangular slabs. We screeched with laughter.

'Not like that! You even *know* the shape of your own mouth?'

But Miri wasn't listening. She stood amongst the graves, out-staring her face in the mirror, like a madwoman eyeballing children on a bus. We laughed, and laughed, until our breath ran out; and then we stopped.

Miri lowered her hand. The mirror dropped out of her palm, into the grass. She stepped forward, and we heard it crack under her heavy shoes. She walked right up to the war memorial and knelt down on it, paused, head bent so low she touched the marble with her forehead, it looked like prayer. But then she straightened her back, held the blood red lipstick over the surface and began to scrawl. She didn't even look down at her hand, she just wrote. Her handwriting was large like an infant, but the words were grown up: *In the beginning was the word and ... The wages of sin are death. Vengeance is mine ... I will bring ruin on those ruining the earth.* She scrawled until the lipstick was flat and the edge of the tube scraped the marble.

We cussed at the waste of a good lipstick.

'What you do that for?' we asked.

'The girl crazy,' we said.

'And *she* the one complaining that we thieve from the dead!'

It started like the edge of rain when you don't even recognise that it's raining. But then the drops fall fatter, fall heavy, fall fast, until you realise you're in a storm and it's too late to find shelter. No-one remembers who was first.

We reached into our pockets, into our bags, and pulled out the small glass stones we'd taken earlier from the graves. We threw the red, blue, white, glass-hard bullets at Miri as she kneeled down on the memorial. At first she flinched and instinctively put her hands up over her face, but then she stood up, swaying. The heat of the day, so soporific earlier, now fuelled our irritation and restlessness. We pounced. Miri was lost underneath our hands and legs as we kicked and punched, still it didn't satisfy, so someone pulled at her shirt, neat buttons popping into the cemetery undergrowth, another girl tore at her skirt. We laughed at her wide girdle-like knickers and pinched bruises into her thighs and fleshy parts.

Delight: malicious, malevolent, pure. We knew the expression our face wore, because we could see it reflected in each other, girl to girl to girl, like a living hall of mirrors. We had only one face.

Miri didn't scream or try to fight back. She clutched ineffectively at her torn shirt and skirt, simultaneously trying to shield herself from our blows. She made no sound other than the deep gasping of her breath, which made her shudder the way someone does when they've finished crying and are now trying to speak. The frenzy that overtook us was brief and as it started to dissipate we fell back, but threw sod at her, dirt lodging under our nails beneath peeling varnish as we pulled up lumps of grass and weed from the ground with our fingers. Even that became wearisome, our arms grew tired, our hands slippery with sweat. Miri had now buckled to the ground, and was a curl of scratches and torn uniform lain down on the marble memorial, framed by her smudged lipsticked words. Her body moved with the convulsions of her silent sobs.

Our own breath was heavy too and we sat or stood, utterly spent, waiting for our breathing to return to silence. We heard the crack of a dry twig behind us. The wild woman of the cemetery was standing there in her dirty denim, staring at us. It wasn't clear if she'd just arrived or if she'd been there watching us all along. 'You girls,' she said. We waited. 'You girls...' she repeated, in her smoke-tar voice, but then she turned her head sideways as if she'd noticed something else, like a bird or a rustling tree, or else she had forgotten she was talking to us. After a while, she looked back, and noticed Miri again.

'Your friend needs a bit o' cleaning up, I reckon.' She took a swig from the can she still carried and turned around and walked away.

The shame of her adult indifference was worse than if she had castigated us, threatened us with the police, or expulsion.

'Get up Miri,' we said, but we said it as if we were the kind ones.

Miri didn't move, so we went over to her and gently pulled her up. She was bleeding where some of the stones had caught her skin. Her torn white blouse was streaked pink with lipstick and blood, and the strange lipstick stripes she had painted over her mouth now reached from ear to ear. Her eyes were red-rimmed, her breathing punctuated by hiccups.

We pulled off her torn school-shirt and covered her with her blazer, over her vest. We saw she was wearing a bra, but pretended not to notice. We walked her back to school, slowly because she was limping, and slipped into the toilets, where we cleaned her up at the sinks. We bathed her cuts. We combed out her hair. We washed her face like Veronica wiping the face of Jesus and lent her concealer, and smudged shadow around her eyes to balance out their bloodshot appearance.

The heat broke that afternoon. The sky grew dark so that it looked like night. From our classroom, we listened to the thunder. There was a flash of lightning over the school, another roll of thunder, and then it started to rain, sudden and heavy. In the space of half an hour it was over. The sky cleared.

Miri didn't come to class the next day nor any day after that until school broke up for the summer two weeks later. We stopped meeting up on Saturdays, and we drifted off across the city, some of us looking after younger brothers or sisters, some of us going to summer playschool, or to stay with cousins or aunts. By the time the new school year started in September, we could hardly recognise each other, our faces and bodies had become unmoulded from their familiar forms. Miri would walk past one, two, many of us at various times; in the corridor, or at the dinner queue. We heard rumours from other girls about how she was always getting into trouble; back-chatting teachers, skipping school, not wearing uniform. She was seen eating packets of bacon crisps. She click-clacked in stilettoes that exaggerated the height she had gained over the summer, swinging her bag over the shoulder of her leather jacket, while her skirt, rolled up at the waist to make it shorter, tilted from side to side over her swaying rear. She walked on without once turning to look at us, and we watched her disappear into the distance.

CRAZY PAVING

Rob Walton

When I was younger, so much younger than today

ALICE LOVED GARDENING AS MUCH AS I DID. RAINFALL ON A TULIP, THE careful removal of a dandelion's tap root, the timely sowing of sweet peas to get an early crop. We were blessed with a passion for the same things, and a passion for each other. We were on the same wavelength. We could use a phrase like 'on the same wavelength' and we'd both follow it with exactly the same movement of our eyebrows. they oscillated in the same way.

We started gardening at number 6. When we wanted – when we *needed* a bigger garden we moved to number 18. Five houses between them, but a gardener's world of difference. We took great pride in moving everything ourselves. Every piece of furniture, every box of books was carried by our once-fair hands. Each carefully-wrapped piece of crockery was conveyed by our good selves. Finally, at a given and agreed signal, and with a spring in our step, we shouldered hoe (Alice) and edging spade (me) and marched the forty metres to the place where we intended to spend the rest of our gardening lives.

We immediately attended to the shrubs. One of our first

jobs, before unpacking the kettle and our gardeners' mugs, was finding the right spot for the bush peony. We knew it was a danger: they're notorious for not liking being moved. We moved it. It didn't like it.

An abnormality showed on Alice's smear test that same summer. We couldn't quite comprehend. We were too young.

Don't interrupt the sorrow

Mike and Fran moved in to number 18 when the floundering man moved out. The woman at Russell, Taylor & John, when she wasn't extolling the virtues of the spacious corner plot, had referred to him as a widower. She believed he wanted a quick sale at a reasonable price, and had no interest in haggling. Mike and Fran had never met him. He had always chosen to be out on their viewings. Any questions were relayed through the estate agent. They had, however, seen his image on a photo on the mantelpiece. A couple in their 40s, leaning on garden spades and squinting into the sunlight. It was difficult to tell if it was taken in the garden of this house they were contemplating buying. In a few months' time it would be impossible to tell.

We decided, as we walked through the corridors after seeing the consultant that everything she had said would have no effect on our plans for the garden. We had – the thing with the eyebrows again – a vision for the garden, and we even laughed when we got in the lift. A couple already there, holding hands and looking down, bowed their heads even further, squeezing their hands until the white showed.

The new occupants of the semi on the corner took to lifting the shrubs and bushes in the front garden straight away. They had an appointment with a block paving firm and wanted to be sorted as soon as possible. They had no intention of on-street parking. They had been warned that sometimes 'your' space was taken by complete strangers and you had to park round the corner or even a couple of streets away. They could not entertain the possibility of being so far away from their car. Besides, if it was parked on what was once the garden, they would be able to keep an eye on it. The chances of vandalism would be reduced substantially.

They paved paradise and put in a parking lot

We watched the birds together and started keeping some sort of journal or diary. Alice bought the thickest notebook I had ever seen. We didn't write a title on it, didn't call it the Bird Journal, it wasn't our Spotting Diary. We started writing and drawing on the first page and carried on, pretty much taking it in turns. When Alice died, the book – we always referred to it as The Book – was very nearly full. I thought about doing something significant and meaningful in the last few pages, but thought the most meaningful thing would be to leave it. Leave the blank pages, where nothing would ever be written or drawn. Meaning is meaning; significance is significance. You don't manufacture it.

What am I supposed to do now?

There is a notion some people have of growing plants because they're practical and 'earn their keep'. These people often have no aesthetic considerations. Alice and I wouldn't have that. We had little interest in that part of Morris's dictum about keeping only things that were useful. Beauty in the garden was the thing with us and, as I mentioned, we beheld beautiful things in much the same way.

The *useful* elements of gardening – fruit, vegetables and herbs – were grown on an allotment we shared with a young couple we rarely saw. The council had paired us together and the system worked well. We decided they must do their gardening on the way home from the pub. It got done but we never saw them doing it. Perhaps they were keeping out of the way of our love. Or, later, perhaps they thought they might catch our bad luck.

We did however have a small pear tree – Onward by name – because I liked the blossom and imagined putting a bench under it one day. The neighbours had a compatible pear tree so pollination would work well and the fruit would be good. I ate the pears only once. They didn't taste right.

We ended up having a year of useful gardening time. We took it and did what we could.

The planning for the garden was done on the hoof – on the wellington as Alice once said. A rockery was clearly ridiculous. We built one. A high-maintenance border with constantly changing seasonal bedding made no sense. It was planted.

We kept ourselves going with our plans. Our worst moments were with two rowan trees we planted. Neither of us could escape the information in the catalogue about how long they would mature, how many years they would be with us.

Mike and Fran had both grown up in houses with gardens. With plants carefully tended by adults as the children played on the lawn. At times they both thought of their childhoods and their childhood gardens. At times snatches of the songs of their youth were on their lips and on their tongues. They tended to swallow them and get on with the difficult business of being a grown-up.

After Alice's death there were days when I was focussed. I would go in the garden at first light and stay out there most of the day. There were also days when I drifted. On the drifting days I would often do nothing other than sit in my armchair and look through The Book. I wouldn't be reading and looking at it the whole time; I'd read a bit, then let my mind go to work on it, think it through. Those days would end with me realising I hadn't eaten, springing up and walking to the Chinese take-away.

'Plain chow mein and chips, Keith?'

A nod.
'Please.'

I'd take a detour on the way home to pick up a bottle or two of beer. I was one of the men – one of the many – who told themselves it was better to do this than always have some in the cupboard or fridge at home.

I'd promise myself not to have any more days like these. Then a few days later I'd find myself in the same chair with The Book open.

Close my eyes and drift away

There were many difficult things I had to cope with, to come to terms with, but the move was the one that did for me. I could cope with leaving the house, that collection of rooms where we'd done all those things. Those memories could come with me quite easily and in a relatively pain-free way. It was leaving the garden that was hard. I stayed in the house for three years before I gathered the courage to move away. I sometimes feel I should have moved further and sooner. I walk past the old house on a regular basis, and it does me no good. No good at all.

Lifting the shrubs and bushes at the front was difficult. Mike and Fran were determined to remove all the roots so there was no chance of any resurgent growth upsetting the block paving. Mike had plans for dwarf conifers in pots on either side of the front door. He had seen the glazed ultramarine pots he wanted and his parents had offered to buy them as a housewarming present.

The new couple – their names were on the papers, but I chose not to look at them – didn't move in straight away. They obviously had other things to do. They had their schedule, they had their own agenda. Their furniture and other belongings arrived, but they were making changes – the woman at the estate agents mistakenly referred to them as 'improvements' – before they stayed there for the first time.

When their furniture van arrived I looked for the boxes marked 'Books', but couldn't see them. Perhaps they would arrive separately.

Fran was particularly happy with the block paving. It was the sort with a wet-look glaze. It always looked particularly fresh and clean, unsullied. The new glazed front door which followed meant they could see it every time they went through the hall, and they could also keep an eye on the car. The house and its surroundings were being knocked in to shape, were working out as they had planned.

One day the postman pushed a manila envelope through the letter box and looked through the triple glazing as it landed neatly and squarely on the map, the hospital department logo very distinct.

The new couple had removed the shrubs so they could put in block paving. Alice and I had made a crazy paving path once. There was a time when paths were made from broken paving slabs. It seems odd to think that such a thing was fashionable. We had a neighbour who bought new slabs and broke them.

This new couple kept one corner which wasn't paved, but

51

it was very clearly defined. One tiny bit of soil, a tiny quadrant, a quarter circle which wasn't paved. The natural world tamed, beaten into a corner, corralled, put under control.

And at one point I was heartened because I saw something creeping over the bricks. I could have told them it would grow quickly and send out runners. It was softening the edge as some gardeners might say, making it all a little bit more natural. The next day it had been primly cut back, so that you could see the contrast in the two different colours of paving stone. It was all under control again.

Mike and Fran hired a skip. Filling it wasn't a task they enjoyed and in many ways they had to steel themselves, but they had come here to start a new life. They hoped for a change of luck. They wanted everything to be fresh and clean, fresh and clean-cut. There was a charming homemade number sign next to the front door. They deliberated long and hard about keeping it, but it eventually went into the skip. Fran had seen some slate ones in B & Q that she liked the look of. They reminded her of that slate mining museum they'd been to – where was it? Wales? The Lake District?

I noticed a skip outside the house. In one of the shrubs, as though it had nested there, was the number 18 sign Alice had made in the shed. A term at woodworking night school the winter after her diagnosis resulted in many things which were in use in that house for the next few years. Alice took herself off to the shed one weekend and carved a number. I proudly held it while she proudly screwed it to the wall.

Carving wasn't something she'd been formally taught, but she found she had a knack for it.

I climbed the skip, leaned over and reached for the sign, and took it to the bungalow. I no longer live at number 18, but there's a place for devilment in the life of a widower. I was attempting to *jolly myself along.*

A few days later I rescued the shrub itself from the skip. I then realised I had nowhere to put it, or not many options, as my bungalow had a tiny rear garden, and a concrete area at the front. I spent a Saturday in early summer with a lump hammer and cold chisel, smashing and chipping away at the paved postage stamp in front of the bungalow, before planting the shrub and giving it a good watering. I thought of a bush peony. I thought of hearing sad news from doctors. Whatever grows is a sign of hope, I told myself, plants are something to get up for. I was very tired after the chipping and digging and had to take an early night. Alice would have smiled and said I was bushed.

Yesterday I felt so old

Passers-by had always found it difficult to see in to the back garden of 18 Enderby Road. In Alice and Keith's time this had been because of the dense planting, the lush foliage with something in leaf in every season. Now, in Fran and Mike's time, it was because of the tight vertical wooden fence panels. They did the job. There would be no conversations over the garden fence. Fran and Mike hoped the pyracantha they had planted because of its anti-burglar properties, would grow as a hedge, but for now the fence was making a statement.

I noticed they had erected a wooden fence with panels which were very close together. They seemed to be on some sort of mission. But there was a clematis *Nelly Moser* squeezing through the gaps, determined to find the light and to spread some colour into people's lives, refusing to accept the flat grey-brown expanse of the fence as how things should be. Within days it was joined by others and then inevitably by flowers.

The next time I walked past they were spraying the fence with some sort of preservative. They sprayed straight over the blooms. She didn't look as though she was enjoying it, almost looked as though it was something she had to do. I thought, and this is probably fanciful, that there was some sort of anger in her. At what I didn't know – flowers? Fences?

Death and birth and death and birth

Mike looked out of the living room window and saw a couple of his age pushing a buggy; hooked over one of the handles was a *Toys R Us* bag. He pulled the cord which closed the blinds.

One day the skip was gone, and their car was parked in front of the house, on the block paving. The car, for some reason, had eyelashes surrounding the headlights.

On another day a second skip arrived. The following morning the shed, which used to be both workshop and potting shed, was dismantled and thrown in the skip. I watched much of this happen. The woman turned to look at me at one point – I was stationary and staring – so I walked on. I instinctively bowed my head with embarrassment, but then remembered the carvings Alice had made in the shed and lifted my head again.

Within days the panes of greenhouse glass were being stacked against the wall, catching the sunshine. The next day some of them had been smashed. I looked at the shattered glass and cast my mind back to when we were putting it up and a pane broke. I thought I was being very calm and cool about it, said we'd finish it the next day and went to do some gardening. Alice went out on her bike straight away and returned from the glazier's an hour later. A pane of glass was somewhat precariously strapped to her bike basket. I smiled for a long time when I saw her. We finished the greenhouse, had a light tea, and enjoyed an early night.

The postman watched Fran sorting through the mail, finding the manila envelope and letting the other letters fall to the floor. It looked as though she was scared to open it.

When they had been in number 18 a few months, they had removed the plants Alice and I grew, paved over the front garden, dismantled the shed and greenhouse and erected a huge fence round the outside of the back garden.

Insult was then added. I walked past and saw their bins in a neat row. They had thoughtfully placed some of the shrubs from the back garden in the 'green' recycling bin rather than hiring another skip. A fortnight later the bins, standing on the block paving, had been covered in adhesive plastic. The designs were grass dotted with daisies, daffodils and a profusion of blossom. The last one was quite indistinct because it had a strange repeated pattern, but it looked as though it could be pear blossom. The following week the bin for the 'green' waste was no longer there. It had done its job and the council had presumably taken it away.

A toddler, clutching a bright orange soft toy giraffe, hid behind Mike and Fran's wall. Her dad, carrying an Early Learning Centre bag, ran round the corner, laughing, pretending he didn't know where she was.

Who knows where the time goes

On bright, sunny days Alice was in my thoughts. On grey, rainy days Alice was in my thoughts.

You are my sunshine, my only sunshine

On the way back from their final visit to the fertility clinic Mike and Fran's car was shunted by an angry impatient man in a black Volkswagen. He gave his details but offered no apology. As he walked away they held hands and looked at each other. Mike shed a solitary tear as they squeezed hands until the white showed.
On the day when I saw a blue car parked on the drive with the words *Courtesy Vehicle supplied by Kay's Accident Repair*

written on its doors my step was a little quicker as I made my way home to make my cup of tea. When I took the tea bag out I used the teaspoon to tap a rhythm on the side of the cup.

Fran opened the door and put a charity bag on the doorstep. It contained a bulky shape, looking like limbs and a head. She returned a moment later to push the brown furry head into the bag and hurriedly taped it up.

I was in my new place one night when I recalled something. I had walked past our old neighbour's many times, but it suddenly dawned on me that their pear tree was no longer there. This puzzled me, and I found it hard to sleep that night. I wandered from room to room, looking without understanding. I suddenly felt I could comprehend nothing. I wandered all night, staring, staring.

All the house lights left up bright

On a cold Tuesday Mike drove the car on to the block paving and thought he heard one of the blocks move. Keith knew one of the blocks was loose because he had stared at it various times over the last week. He thought of knocking and telling them, introducing himself.

And so it was that on the following Saturday Keith picked up the loosened block and approached the door of number 18 with a mess of thoughts in his head. The door opened before he got there. Fran looked at a man holding a brick and Keith looked at a woman on her doorstep. Something crumpled in both of them.

PICNICKING WITH MY FATHER

Shelley Day Sclater

IN THE NIGHT THE SMELL OF ENGINE OIL, MY FATHER HERE TO fetch me.

Howay wor lass, it's time to come. His voice, soft as the dark, cradles my head like a pillow. I feel the rough stubble of his chin against my cheek as he bends over and scoops me up. I'm limp, the Lady of Shalott, pale hair, pale limbs, trailing. The sweet oniony smell of sweat is on my father's shirt and I hear the soft thud thud thud of his heartbeat.

My father will take me to the river, which is where he comes from and where I like to go.

My teacher will say: *Does anyone know the Ouseburn area?* and I'll say, *Yes, me, I do! My father takes me there. For picnics.*

Liar! Maureen chips in.

She's a liar, her. Her dad's in prison. He doesn't take her nowhere.

But what does she know? It had been easier to let them all think he'd gone to jail. They think what they like anyway.

What my mother says is good bloody riddance and I haven't even got the sense I was born with. My sister's been picked for the swimming team and it's all she ever thinks about. My nanna can't be doing with palaver and anyway it's

59

Wednesday; I should be holding my tongue and cleaning out the grate.

I clean out the grate on Wednesdays because that's the day my nanna's ladies come. Jenny Bingham isn't allowed to touch a thing; only me. I open the lid on the piano. I lift the geraniums down one by one from the little table in the bay; I squeeze a leaf between thumb and forefinger, sniff the peppery smell. I pull the table into the middle of the room taking care not to ruck the carpet. I put on a clean white cloth and smooth it with the flats of my hands. Then the board and the glass and the three candles, and the five chairs all around. It's a bit cramped on one side with two. Then I clean out the grate and set the fire and at seven pm precisely the ladies will arrive and my nanna will put a match to the kindling and woe betides if I haven't put enough paper.

The ladies will nod at each other. They'll take off their coats but leave their hats on and keep their handbags close to. They'll pull on the white cotton gloves and they'll have a little sing with thin voices before they get started.

Afterwards it'll be candles out and lights on and tea in the primrose cups. After they've gone, there'll be a lingering smell of lavender water and mothballs. And in the morning the sweet dark smell of soot.

My mother says what a load of old baloney and hasn't she got better things to do.

I won't be doing the grate this Wednesday though. I'll be down by the river, skimming stones, doing cartwheels, picking monkey flowers. Picnicking with my father.

My father always sits on the bank and smokes his pipe

while I look around and gather things. He lifts his chin up to suck smoke in then glides it out and goes pup pup pup like a guppy only more lop-sided. He can be like that for hours. I have plenty of time for doing anything. I could wander off and sometimes do, but never far. There's no point; there's everything I could ever want, right there by the river.

You'd be amazed at the things the old river throws up: mangled bits of metal, chipped green bottles half stuffed with mud, pieces of china, spangled spikes of coloured tin. My favourite: Balls that would have been other children's, now bashed in and half deflated, faded rubber cracked and perished, but still floating. Really that's what makes things special: all those imperfections. You can't help but wonder about the lives they must have had.

They find me down by the river in my flannenette nightie. My sewing teacher will say, *Excuse me, I think you'll find it's flannelette*, and I'll say, *Oh, I'm sorry*. But I won't mend my ways. I've no intention of mending my ways. She imagines that I stand corrected.

They find me at the river's edge wearing the flannenette nightie that reaches the ground. They say I am Wee Willy Winkie except I am shuddering with cold. Mud has squeezed up between my toes and dried crusty on the tops of my feet. I watch them mouthing Hush Child and hear the hiss of whispers; they say I'll have caught my death. My father has already gone. He knows when he's not welcome.

He has to go before they come because he's not approved of and neither is the Ouseburn which is dirty with rats and typhoid and leeches. All my father leaves is the smell of engine oil down by the viaduct, where the lead-works and the lime kiln and the pottery used to be, and the great black barges carried coal.

Even my grandmother's ladies don't want my father, or at least that's what they'll have me believe. Sometimes he's all I can get and then they have to make do because beggars can't be choosers. Anyway, I can't choose my baggage any more than they can, and well they know it. But they'd much rather not have him; they say so quite openly: *We'd rather not have you again Mr Robson, if anyone else is available. Is there anybody there?*

The ladies concentrate into the special prayer of protection; they breathe slowly and deliberately, their old eyelids flickering almost shut, their old hands in the white cotton gloves splayed open on the table, pinkie touching pinkie, thumbs pressed together.

They find me down at the river and they wrap me in sheets because it's all they have, or it seems the best thing, I'm not sure which. They carry me so my legs dangle and my feet are suspended above the ground. It's as though I'm hovering, as though I could float away. They bring me back to the house; I'm tilted and jolted as they make their way up the steep back steps where dried up stalks of rose bay willow herb and long snatches of bramble have died scrambling among rubble and stones. I keep my eyes shut and feel the ladies flinch when the thorns snag at their stockings and they're wishing they weren't having to carry me.

Well they didn't have to. I could have found my own way back as I've done many times before, gliding back by myself under the moonlight, my little stockinged feet barely brushing the cobbles dull pale with frost. Unlike those ladies, I wouldn't let my shoes slither on the fine green moss that coats the stone. At the old back door I wouldn't need to fumble and fuss with the fat iron key that objects as soon as it feels the warmth of a hand. It occurs to me as they push at the door with their skinny shoulders just how burdensome their lives are.

The door cracks then creaks open and I'm almost uprighted in the haste and being borne across the empty hall. Clack cleck clack clack echo the stout shoes on the parquet. Swish swush swish go the cold skirts, wafting strict smells of carbolic and starch. Which of these ladies in the white cotton gloves is successful in stifling a pall-bearing thought?

I won't open my eyes until they've unravelled my sheets, put on my white cotton gloves, set me down at my place at the table, and splayed open my hands.

It's mostly dark where you have to go on Wednesdays. They think you don't mind, but you do, and they can't know you do. What *they* want is what matters, and you go along with it, you go along with it, because there isn't any other way, not really. Today the ladies exhale the smells of dentures and mints. It's not unpleasant, but they forget how sensitive you are, even to these small things. They don't know how thin your skin is, how hardly even visible, stretched as it is over your filigree of vital purple veins like an unborn child. They can't know the terrible weight of the longing that seeps out of their fond little mouths, that squeezes between their teeth, from under their soft wet tongues, through lips drawn back tight and dispelling. They're sucking teeth and mints and swallowing sin and spitting out prayer and they're expecting you to catch it all and carry it all: the weight of words. Well you can't. You can't.

With the best will in the world, no-one can.

One day you'll take them to the ruined Mill. Down at the Mill you've sat with your father and you've picked armfuls of yellow flag irises and monkey flowers and you've laid them on the bank. Or, like today, you've tucked your skirt into your knicker legs and paddled in, oops, oops, slipping, sliding on stones slime green with algae, almost but not quite losing your footing, you hold yourself up with wavered outstretching of your arms. *Gan canny, bonny lass,* your father says, *divven't gan fallin in.* You look up. You hadn't known he was there today, or that he was watching. But you're glad he is, and you realize this is what you'd been hoping for: whatever else is this sliding silly performance on algae, on stones that cut your feet, in this stinking river milky with death, what else is it all about?

You will cross. You will cross the river to the other side, to where your father waits.

You're very cold but nearly half way there, getting towards the middle where there'd be no point in turning back. Your father is waiting and he was man and boy by this filthy river and his father before him and his before that, all of them man and boy while the foundries smoked and the glassworks smoked and the flint mill and the flour mill and the flax mill and the molten lead squeezed flat in the rolling mill and the smoke sank low all around the viaduct and down down around where the little houses crouched in tight together. Man and boy.

For you, now, the Ouseburn is a rubicon of leeches that suck at your ankles, that attach, glutinous, gluttonous, sticking until you dislodge them with sharpened sticks. Further in and the opaque grey water gushes round your thighs and it's hard to stay standing even with your feet in mud. Your skirt's come out at the back and it's soaked and slapping at your bare wet legs. Behind you the wind makes the thin trees wince and growls hungry at the Mill with its crumbling stone and gaping black windows, empty eyes watch as you march on, more slowly now, your thigh muscles braced to push against the water. Your father is there, holding out his hands.

When the river reaches your waist you stretch up your arms into the air, your thin red skirt lashes around you as if trying to escape. Then the river is gripping your chest and for a moment you are a ballet dancer pirouetting pirouetting, catching glimpses of everything all run in together. You hear the wind and the rush of the wild river thrashing. The river tumbles you and tumbles you and then you are floating. Shreds of your red skirt froth into the culvert where you come to rest.

The guide-book says: Once a cradle of industrialisation, the Ouseburn Valley is a now a cultural hub, well worth a visit. It has a regeneration trust and some original industrial buildings. There are riding stables, studios, shops and galleries, and real ale and music to be had every night at The Cluny.

My father and I laugh. We say: Look, look at the filthy Ouseburn that refuses to be gentrified. We sit side by side down under the viaduct and we skim stones and we eat our picnic.

THE HOUSE

Eileen Jones

IT WAS SQUARE. SQUARE WINDOWS AND SQUARE ROOMS — A HOUSE
with a corner at every corner. It was a brick box on an estate
that more than forty years on, people still called 'new' with
a sneer in their voice. It was a house a bored child might
have drawn, or built from Lego. It had no interesting nooks
or quirks and its period features were an old thug of a gas
boiler, naked pipes, greasy lino tiles, and cracks. Cracks in
the plaster, cracks in the ceilings and windowsills and a half
inch gap between the upper floors and the skirting boards.

It was a flaking blemish on a well groomed street, but the
house nudged at me all the same. Light poured in through
the big plain windows and the views over the valley were,
in the favourite word of the estate agent, 'stunning'. There
was even something satisfying about the way every room was
square. Built in the brash days of moon travel, before the
mock Georgian excesses of the late seventies, the house had
attitude: a 'won't-impress-yer-arty-pals' cockiness.

I asked a builder to look round it with me. His face lit up
like a lottery winner's.

'Location,' he said, 'and position, that's what you have to
go for. And it hasn't been mucked around – there's been no
cowboys in it.'

Not yet, I thought, searching his honest, open features. But he knew his stuff. He told me why the bedroom floors – 'proper wood floors' – had dropped: something technical about an absent supporting beam.

I liked his certainty. Nothing was a major problem, not even the one improvement made by the previous owners: the removal of the kitchen cupboard that kept the landing up. I should have made a run for it, but I looked into Don's hazel eyes and instead of pound signs I saw something foolish and seductive: enthusiasm. He couldn't wait to get at that house: couldn't wait to strip it, shore it up, fill in the cracks and make it decent with a clean white bath and a scrubbed Swedish kitchen. I checked the agent's details again. Once I'd translated: 'scope for updating', and 'realistic asking price', into: 'neglected shack, going cheap', they were accurate enough. I noticed it had been built in the year I started school. That seemed significant. Rid of their respective interior clutter, this house and my life could be remade.

Of course, I had my doubts – experience had made me wary of attempting rescues. But this was only a house.

'It seems a bit damp,' I said.

'Bound to be. Been standing empty for six months. Not a major problem.'

At weekends, I would go and see how Don and the lads were doing. It was raining the first time, like it had been for weeks. As I parked outside I saw water splashing over the bricks from a point above the bathroom window.

Don came to the door when I called out. He looked up at

the spurting water, unperturbed. 'We'll get on to that when the rain stops,' he said.

There was a skip on the road outside, full of old radiators, washbasins, a toilet pan, rancid floor tiles and naked pipes. I felt a pang when I looked at it, like I was responsible for ripping the guts out of something.

At first sight, Don's team were as unpromising as the house. The Old Feller was pale grey and tiny, and at least ten years older than Don. He had the large-framed glasses and mild manner of a serial killer. The Lad was well over six feet tall with a spotty neck, shorn-off blond hair, and an expression of deep disenchantment. I only saw him animated once: he'd sneaked out to the garden to send a text and he was loitering by the broken shed, giggling.

The work got done all the same, and it got done properly – Don was a strict gaffer in his quiet way. After the first miserable week, the sun shone down on the lads without a break. By the end of a month the house had smart new drainpipes and window frames, and the toothy gaps in the roof ridge had been capped. Inside, the plaster was wedding-cake smooth, the joiner was fitting the granite work tops, and the oak flooring would arrive any day. I didn't doubt the quality of the work. I had absolute faith in Don by then.

But on one luminous May evening I looked around the sunny kitchen before I went out to the car, and I knew that something was amiss. The sharp smells of drying plaster and new wood seemed as promising as the warm earth and drifting blossom outside, but I sensed a sulky, jarring note. The house seemed like one of those unconvinced and self-conscious makeover victims on a TV fashion show – the ones who say, 'Of course, I'd never have chosen this myself...'

On the Sunday of the fifth week, it rained again. There was thunder and lightning before I left the city and I drove the twenty miles to the house in a downpour. I parked opposite and I was about to dash to the front door, when I noticed water cascading from that same spot above the bathroom window.

Don looked perplexed when I pointed it out. 'Don't understand it,' he said, 'the joint must have sprung apart.'

I could see he was embarrassed; he'd put in the new gutters himself.

'Well,' I said, 'not a major problem is it?'

The following week, rain seeped in through a window frame; the cold water tank dripped its contents through the light fitting into the living room; and three of the shiny new radiators peed on to the – luckily still unpolished – floorboards. Don was looking more and more depressed. It was my turn to be reassuring. Only The Old Feller and The Lad were unphased. I suppose they didn't mind a bit of overtime fixing problems that weren't their fault.

I arrived one afternoon and was amazed to hear Don shouting. He was on the phone to the plumber. The third plumber. The previous two had been sacked after the disasters with the heating system.

Don had been gutted about the first one: 'Can't understand it. I've worked with him for years.'

As soon as I walked into the dining room, the latest

calamity was obvious. The new ceiling was bowed and split and The Lad was half-heartedly mopping up the lake beneath it. The Old Feller told me he'd filled the new bath before sealing its edges and when he'd pulled the plug the water had flooded out of the unconnected drain.

Don was still sitting on the stairs yelling into his mobile. He dropped the phone and swore again. Then he looked up at me. 'Sorry,' he said. Under his tan, his neck was pink with rage and embarrassment. 'I've got high standards you know. I'm not cheap but I do a good job. Anybody would tell you. I could give you names, phone numbers, show you letters – '

'It's OK, 'it's not –' but I stopped myself from saying it. Instead, I found his thermos in the kitchen and poured him a cup of coffee – ground coffee by the smell of it. Don had high standards for everything.

And then the rain stopped again and it all came together at last. The removal van turned up on time, everything got hooked up and switched on, the new bed and sofa arrived undamaged and three weeks after the bath debacle I was living in the house. My cousin and her husband helped me with some of the unpacking and all of the getting hammered afterwards and I flopped into my new bed, looking forward to my first weekend in my new home.

I woke up less than an hour later, listening. It took me a few seconds to work out where I was. And then I lay still, trying to identify the sounds. There was the washer, of course, still chomping away at the curtains I'd shoved into it last night, and there were the creaks houses make that you only hear after dark, as if they're shifting and settling in their sleep. But these creaks were more like the shuffling of a fractious caged animal.

I never told Don about the flood I found in the kitchen the next morning. After all, it was nothing to do with him. I should have replaced that old washing machine – and the insurance were surprisingly quick about sorting out the floor. It was all put right by the end of the week and by the following weekend I was fully unpacked and tidied up. I went out and treated myself to a framed print that went with everything in the living room. The swirling colours were glorious, although I was a bit taken aback when I read the title on the label.

Don's final bill arrived on the Saturday. It was steep, but I knew he couldn't have made much out of it – with all the setbacks he'd have been lucky to cover his costs. I was about to stick a stamp on the envelope when I had second thoughts.

He recognised my voice straight away. He sounded anxious. 'Everything alright?'

'Fine. Would you like to call round for your cheque? If you've got time? See the finished effect?' I asked him to bring the lads along too.

But I was pleased when he came on his own. Scrubbed up he looked younger. His thick hair was darker without the plaster dust. I was wearing a summer dress instead of old jeans. Nothing flash, but it was new. We were awkward with each other at first, but only until we started on the house tour. I was pleased he liked my print, and that he laughed when I told him what it was called. During all the pear-shaped weeks of our acquaintance, neither of us had had much reason to laugh. And on the better days, he'd still been intent on his work – friendly enough, but preoccupied. I was glad to see the square lines of his face soften for once.

Later, we sat on the modest York stone patio in the July sunshine and drank a glass of the Condrieu I'd been saving for a special occasion.

He was impressed: 'This must be pricey?'

'My ex was in the wine business. This was his parting gift.'

'Very civilised.'

'He didn't think so.'

'Sorry?'

'When he spotted it was missing.'

He drained his glass and stared into it before he put it down on the white table and smiled at me. It felt strange, him looking me straight in the eye like that. I was used to him speaking to me over his shoulder, calling down from the top of a ladder, or pointing something out on a ceiling or skirting board.

A few drops of water splattered on to the striped cotton above our heads and we leaned back to peer at a threatening sky.

'Better get inside,' I said, 'its going to chuck it down.'

'I suppose I should be getting back,' he said.

I felt a bit awkward. I realised I knew hardly anything about him: I wasn't sure what he'd be getting back to – where he lived, what sort of house he had, and who he shared it with. Did I want to know? And did I want him to stay longer?

'How about a coffee before you go? Help me christen the

new espresso machine? I know you like proper coffee.'

What the hell, I thought, he could easily say no.

But he didn't; he trotted into the kitchen with something close to eagerness and helped me lift the heavy machine out of the cupboard.

'It was a housewarming present.' I said, and added 'from my brother,' suddenly anxious to make it clear that I hadn't stocked the whole house at my ex-husband's expense. Fat chance.

'Gaggia? Brilliant. I used to have one. No room for it now though.' He set about assembling the parts of the machine, then prised open the coffee tin and meticulously levelled off the little scoop. I watched, fascinated. It was a different task from fixing gutters, but his long, tanned fingers looked just as expert.

'Can't you extend your kitchen?'

'No,' he said.

No? Perhaps it was the old story of the workman neglecting his own place. Maybe I should just ask him straight out about his living arrangements.

He finished filling the metal container with coffee. Then he turned around and looked at me.

'I live in a caravan,' he said.

We sat in the living room while the coffee brewed and I got the whole story. How he'd always wanted to work with his dad, but the family firm had gone belly-up:

'He tried to build a few decent quality houses – couldn't compete with the big boys and their helicopters and special offers. He didn't want to work for those bastards – so he took a job on a housing co-op –a block of 'studio flats'. Not enough room to swing a gerbil in any of them. And they were rubbish. Matchwood window frames, Weyrock floors and' – he almost spat out the words – *'ceiling heating.* Mum thought it was what killed him – he got so frustrated with it all.'

So Don had set up in a small way on his own, as a property developer, but still trying to stick to his dad's top-quality principles. That's when it struck me that he should have been a cowboy after all: a quiet stranger with a troubled past, riding into some frightened town, locking up the whisky-sodden coward of a sheriff in his own cell, and squaring up, doomed and alone, to the big boys in their black hats. And if he survived, the sheriff's sad-eyed daughter would have to let him go. No woman could keep a man like that from his mission.

But I hadn't got the last bit right. Things hadn't worked out with the business because he'd been let down by his project manager, Lisa. Now he was living alone in a mobile home on the last surviving project – a wreck of a Georgian – real Georgian – farmhouse.

I suppose this was my cue to respond with my own sad history, but I was bored with it – and I reckoned anyone could guess most of it, once they knew that my wine-merchant husband hadn't mastered the crucial art of spitting out.

'Sorry,' Don said. 'It's been great seeing you so happy with the house. I shouldn't moan on. I'm spoiling this nice evening for you.'

'Don't worry,' I said, 'that's not a major problem.'

He looked different when he smiled. It was strange really

– mostly when people don't laugh or smile a lot it looks wrong when they do – like they've stuck on a false nose or something, but with Don, it looked completely right and normal – as if his more usual serious face was the mask.

I felt very close to him – as if we'd dislodged some bricks in the wall between us and anything was possible. Anything we wanted. I had a strong urge to touch him: take his hand or stroke his carefully shaved cheek – no burning passion, no grabbing at anything – just something slow and gradual and subtle.

But Don was out of his chair and bounding upstairs.

I followed him into my bedroom, a bit hesitantly, but he was standing in the corner staring upwards. Water was dripping from the corner of the ceiling. Not a huge amount: just a plink-plink on to the newly polished floorboards. Apparently it wasn't a ... but he didn't say that of course; he said it was just some roofing felt that needed replacing.

'I should have spotted –' he began, but I put my finger over his lips. He helped me mop up and I found an old washing- up bowl to put under the drip. Then we stood for a moment, side by side, looking out of my bedroom window at the rain-blurred hills above the valley.

There was a neatly pressed line in the sleeve of his blue plaid shirt and I wondered how he achieved that in a caravan. I longed to rest my head on his steady shoulder and inhale his reassuring woody scent of plain soap and fresh-air-dried cotton – I thought I could have stayed like that for a long time. But the injured ceiling continued to bleed into the bowl in the corner and I could hear a note of merciless triumph in the uneven pizzicato of the drips.

Don arranged to come back when the rain stopped and after he'd left I made up the single bed in the spare room on the other side of the house.

But I couldn't sleep that night, even though the bed was comfortable and we'd never got round to drinking the coffee. I could still hear the maddening plink of the water in the other room. Eventually I took my duvet downstairs, switched on the TV and found myself gripped by the last half of 'Shane'. As I watched Alan Ladd's wounded and enigmatic stranger riding away from the homesteaders he'd protected and the woman he loved, I realised my eyes were full of tears. I wondered about Lisa, the woman who'd let Don down. He hadn't said so, but I knew she'd been more to him than a project manager.

The rain didn't let up for three days. I had to keep emptying the washing-up bowl and on the third morning I went to get my post and found it floating in a soupy puddle. Twenty minutes later, I abandoned my attempts to mop up. The whole porch was flooded. I couldn't even see where the water was coming in.

Don answered the phone straight away. I tried to sound calm.

'I'll be right round,' he said.

I sat in the living room while he made his inspection. I could hear him splashing around, pulling up floorboards. By the time he'd arrived, the scummy water had started lapping into the hall, and his expression had been easy to read. Now, I found myself staring at a pale map of Africa on the ceiling

– a lingering scar of one of the previous disasters. I felt like I should be chain- smoking. I picked up a magazine then put it down again. It was the latest copy of 'Ideal Home'.

I was picking dead heads off the pelargoniums when Don came in, his face grim. 'There might be water running through the foundations,' he said, 'it might even be a fracture in the main drain – although it doesn't smell too bad, not yet. Whatever it is, it could be a–'

I shook my head. I couldn't bear to hear him say it. And I knew that for once he'd got something wrong. That house didn't have foundations, it had roots. Great twisted, clanking pipes that could tug an underground stream off course or force their way through the yellow clay, and burrow into the flooded mine shafts below us.

Don wanted to tackle the new problem. He put a tentative arm around my shoulders.

'We've come this far,' he said. 'It'd mean a lot to me. And it might *not* be a – we might be able to put it right. Without spending a fortune. '

The warmth of his arm was comforting, but I patted his hand, and stepped aside.

'No,' I said, 'you've got enough to do with your own homestead– home. And this house. It's not meant to be. I've had enough. I need to get away for a while. And when I come back I want a flat. With hermetically sealed windows. A flat in the middle of a block. No roof or foundations. And I'm going to rent.'

He shook his head sadly. 'I've never liked flats, not since...'

'I know', I said.

I advertised the house on the Net. At a 'realistic' price, but enough to pay off the mortgage and leave me with something. And I had a convincing reason for wanting a quick cash sale: my sudden whim to set off round the world as one of the new wave of midlife gappers.

As soon as I'd made my decision to quit, the sun showed up again and the water receded. Don made good the floorboards and the other superficial damage, refusing to accept any payment.

'My parting gift,' he said sadly, 'to make up for all the trouble.'

I kissed him on the cheek. 'You're the best,' I said. But I knew I'd let him down.

The smiling Californian worked for a software company. They had a subsidiary locally and they needed temporary staff homes. There were no probing questions; before you could say 'full structural survey' Silicon Man had given the house and Don's invoices a quick glance, tapped on his smartphone and the deal was sealed.

The night before the sale went through, my cousin took me back to the house for a final check. I was queasy with nerves as I unlocked the front door, but everything was quiet and dry. Perhaps the house had finally slaked its thirst. Not that it was water it thirsted for. Water was just the instrument.

I leaned on the spotless peninsula unit in the kitchen and wondered if hauling the house into the present all the way from the age of Ford Cortinas and Angel Delight had been too much for it. Too much, too late. Had it been brooding all those years, sour and untouched behind its yellowing nets, secretly craving all the 'significant upgrades' of its peers?

I had a vision of nursing it into the 21st century: an accelerated but sensitive evolution via artexed ceilings and avocado bathroom fittings; through phoney dado rails and coving; through smoked glass shelves and black ash coffee tables.

My cousin wandered around the empty rooms. 'You've left the Kandinsky print in the living room. I've always liked that one. What is it again?'

'It's called 'Flood Improvisation'. You can have it if you like.'

We decided to leave it for the new occupants.

She squeezed my hand before we left. 'It's just a house,' she said.

As I closed the gate, I thought I heard a faint tinkle of breaking glass. I had a brief vision of the picture slipping from the living room wall and crashing on to the marble hearth below as the house shrugged off the last remnant of its tormentor. But there was no time to investigate – my cousin had already started the car. As we drove off, I sat in the passenger seat, staring ahead through the pelting rain. I didn't look back.

Tough Love

Avril Joy

IT WAS THE DAY THE BIRDS FELL OUT OF THE SKY. I WAS WASHING UP AT the sink, looking out onto the snow and thinking about Iris. I was thinking about her so much I scraped the burnt remains of the beef casserole into the water and turned it a muddy grey. Pieces of blackened beef floated on the surface in the bubbles.

I felt bad, really bad and I wanted to say sorry.

I lifted my hands out of the washing up bowl and flung off the soapy suds. I would take a walk past her house and see if she was in. I pulled on a pair of old riding boots, my duffle coat and the brown furry hat: my present from Iris. It fastened under the chin and looked like something a child might wear in a school play to impersonate a woodland creature; or something your mother would insist on to keep out the cold. It smelled of chicken feed. I struggled to fasten it, unlike Iris whose fingers had fastened a hundred children's hoods and who would have done it in seconds. I caught sight of myself, owl-like in the mirror. Well, I was wearing it, even if the sun had been powering down at thirty degrees I would still have been wearing it. Why? Because the hat was it: the hat was the reason why Iris had upped and left. And it was all my stupid, vain fault.

Outside weeks of snow had sealed the village. Icicles hung like daggers from the eaves of houses and an east wind blew up from the river across frozen lakes of road and pavement. I set off slowly down the bank towards Grange Farm, thinking about Iris. I thought about how when I met her thirty years ago, she was a sparrow chick with soft downy skin, a brown halo of feathery hair and a tiny mouth. I thought about her laughing, how together we were always laughing, because no matter what was going down, Iris and me, we always found a reason to laugh.

When I moved north to the village, Iris was the first person I spoke to. Ronnie was out at work all day and I was at home. It was his idea, the move. I wasn't so sure myself. I was looking for a librarian's job but I wasn't in a hurry. It was spring and I started digging over the garden, planting lettuce and cornflowers in the fallow black soil.

We hit it off straight away. She would come round when Dennis her husband was out and bring mugs of coffee and stale bread for the birds. I'd stop my digging then and we'd sit on the step drinking coffee, smoking cigarettes and watching the starlings swoop.

I loved Iris but Dennis, he was another matter. For one thing he shouted a lot, well, all the time, especially at Iris and their daughters: Melanie who was six and Leanne who was ten and wasn't his anyway. Once he shouted at Ronnie for parking the car too near his fish van. He had a wild temper Dennis. He made his living buying fish on the quayside at Shields and bringing it back and selling it door to door. He smelled of fish, still does, like all those years selling it impregnated his skin and muscle through to the bone. Anyway that was another reason I didn't much like him: the fishy smell.

When I told Iris that Ronnie and I weren't married she said things like that didn't matter to her but I don't think she ever told Dennis. There were a lot of things Iris kept from Dennis, like how she went to the fortune teller who lived under the viaduct in the hope of being told she hadn't made the biggest mistake of her life in hooking up with him. I could probably have told her for nothing that she had. But what was the point in telling someone something they already knew? We didn't go in for that tough love thing. We never told each other the unpleasant truths, the things we knew without being told, we mostly just stuck to making each other feel the best we could.

'You better come in then,' said Iris opening her back door when she saw me outside on the cinder yard. 'It's bloody freezing. I thought you were staying in away from the cold, you don't want to be bad again.'

'Never mind me. Besides I wanted to come down,' I said stamping my boots on the doormat. 'I wanted to see you.'

'Haway in then,' she said. She didn't call me *unny*, her way of saying *honey*, like she usually did, just ushered me into the kitchen and I sat down in the usual place at the round pine table while she put the kettle on. 'I see you've got it on then.' She didn't hide the smile on her face.

'You were right,' I said, 'it keeps my ears warm, keeps the whole of my head lovely and warm.'

'Yes. Well. That's why I got it.' She put a mug of coffee

down triumphantly in front of me as well as two thickly buttered cream crackers with cheese and then lit up a cigarette, which I thought was funny because Dennis didn't like her smoking and as far as I knew he didn't even know that she did.

'Yes I know,' I said. I took a bite out of one of the crackers, it tasted good. I was glad Iris used butter like paste and I was glad to be in her kitchen.

'Where's Dennis?' I asked, lifting my plate as I bit into the second cracker. Dennis was registered disabled on account of having the bones in his neck fused and it was a rare thing not to see him sat in his chair by the Aga and Iris waiting on him while he issued instructions such as, 'Iris, Iris, tie my shoe laces,' or 'Iris, Iris' – in case she hadn't heard him first time although she was only feet away – 'put my clean socks on.' One night when we sat together in the barn, minding Dennis's sow because she was due to give birth, Iris told me she'd fallen for Dennis because he called her by her name. Her first husband only ever called her *thou*, she said. Once, on a bad day, she told me she'd rather die than hear Dennis shouting her name again.

'Upstairs lying down, the cold's got to his bones.'

Like the fish then, I thought.

Iris stood with her back to me looking out of the kitchen window. 'I hate these dark days, never see the bloody sun. Can't wait for the light nights,' she said. I heard her drag on her cigarette. 'Still won't be long,' she turned to face me with a smile and a sudden upturn in mood.

I didn't like to remind her there were months of winter

ahead, possibly the worst yet to come. I didn't want to spoil
the way she was feeling, the way everything seemed alright
between us. I didn't want to *rain on her parade*. Like I said,
that wasn't our style, especially because both of us in our own
ways, and right from the start, had had a lifetime of people
raining on our parade, mothers especially. We knew about
mothers alright and we knew about kids and about not having
kids and we knew what it was like to want love so badly it got
you to the wrong place.

'Shall I pick you up in the morning?' I said. 'Go into
town for a coffee, look in the Red Cross shop? I need to get a
birthday card and pay a cheque in. We could go in the library
café or Majors you can have a fag out the back there. They've
got a shelter.'

'What time?' said Iris, rattling the coals in the Aga.
She rarely said no to the chance of getting out from under
Dennis's watch.

'Ten?'

'Make it ten thirty. I'm looking after the bairn until ten,
just while Leanne gets to the doctors.' She closed the Aga
door and leaned up against it, warming her behind. 'On
second thoughts, not to worry, Leanne might be late back,
best make it next week sometime.' Then she took a cigarette
from her pocket, didn't get out the air freshener or her mints,
just lit up.

'You sure?'

'Sure, let's go next week. You're going to London aren't
you? We'll go when you get back. And don't forget if the
wind's like it is today, wear your hat.'

'OK Mum. I will.'

'Funny but not funny,' said Iris smiling.

I stepped outside into the wind. Snow fell like pale ash on the cinder yard; and then the birds. They fell like lumps of coal, wings folded, out of the sky and landed with a thump on the cinders disturbing the fresh snow. Starlings: five, six already, and more. One after the other they fell and lay with blood on their beaks and their claws curled in submission. Some flapped their wings lamely, others appeared already dead. I was going to call Iris to come and look, I turned back towards the door, but then I thought better of it.

Me: 'Where's Dennis?' I was back from London and sat in Iris's kitchen drinking coffee.

Iris: 'Gone.'

Me: 'Gone?'

'Yes gone. He's left me.'

'Dennis? Dennis's left *you*?' Me, incredulous. 'Dennis couldn't leave anyone, he can barely walk. His bones are fused. He sits in that chair all day and you have to put his socks on and feed him.'

'Well he has. His sister came and he went with her in her fancy car.'

'I didn't know Dennis had a sister.'

'Probably never mentioned her. Blanche. Lives near Whitby, you know, somewhere near the sea.' Iris sighed, took a cigarette from her packet, held a cardboard taper in the Aga fire and put the flame to her tab end. 'Said he wasn't going to listen to me wittering on all day. Said I was never satisfied, dog with a bone that's me according to him, never let up. So I told him he was shite. The whole thing was shite, biggest mistake I ever made. Fortune teller told me that, not that I needed telling. Next thing I know he's on the phone to his sister, then she turns up and whisks him off. Told him not to bother coming back. I shouted after him, *clear off*, that's what I said. As loud as I could. And he shouted back the same and to get the yard cleared up, you know the dead birds. *Clear them up yourself*, I said. Anyway they're gone now.'

'When was this?' Iris had her back to me. Her cigarette rested in a saucer on the sink side and she was making a second cup of coffee.

'When you were in London.'

'Why didn't you ring me? You should've rung me.' In the past if something bad happened, like the time Leanne was taken into hospital with her asthma, I'd be the first person Iris phoned.

'What for? I'm fine. Better off without him, had a good clear out, cleaned the place top to bottom, even shampooed the carpets.' Iris put a mug of coffee and a buttered scone on the table in front of me. 'Got rid of the birds too. Nice man down at the Reserve, Fergus you call him, knows a lot about birds. He did it for me. Dug a hole. I paid him mind and I said *make it a big one* because that pig of Dennis's died, the one I spent all my time feeding. So I buried the lot: birds and pig, filled the hole in myself. Look at these,' Iris pinched out her cigarette in the ashtray, rolled up the sleeve of her fleece and tensed her muscles.

'OK, wonder woman.' I sipped my coffee. I didn't feel like

87

eating the scone. 'When do you think he'll be back then?'

'He won't be. He's gone for good.'

'But surely his sister won't...'

'Can we talk about something else?' She lit another cigarette and sat down in Dennis's chair next to the Aga. 'How's Ronnie?'

'Same as ever,' I said, 'Never mind Ronnie. What do the girls say?'

'Oh Leanne can't stand him anyway; why should she, he's not her father? And Melanie, well she was a bit upset but she'll get over it. Wants an address for him. Well I haven't got one so I can't help her out there. Anyway now he's gone I can mind the bairns any time and that suits them both. I'm not tied down anymore, am I? Not worrying all the while what he'll say when I get in, or about getting back to make his tea. Anyway,' she said pausing, tilting her head back and blowing smoke into the air, 'I've got an allotment. That Fergus he knows someone on the committee and he got me one just like that.' She clicked her fingers.

'An allotment? Are you mad? You don't want an allotment, all that digging and carting stuff about in wheelbarrows. Why?'

'It's a hobby isn't it? I've got time for hobbies now and when the weather picks up we'll be able to go and sit there. I'm going to get a shed, take the old picnic chairs and table. I'll make a nice flask and we'll be able to sit there in the summer having a cuppa, sweet peas high as a hedge and smelling like talc, birds singing. And I'll be able to smoke to my heart's content.'

'Well if you put it like that. But all that work.'

'Fergus knows someone with a rotavator and I've got stacks of manure. Besides I used to dig my granda's allotment for him. I'm a powerful digger when I set my mind to it. Put your coat back on when you finish that coffee and we'll go down and have a look. I'll show you my patch. It's frozen over now, ground's like concrete but it won't be long before things get warmed up again, then I'll start. You watch, I'll have the best runner beans going.' She lifted her coat from the hook on the back of the door and began to pull it on. 'Dennis hated runner beans, *like a pile of string*, he always said.' She was buttoning up her coat now right to the very top button. She pulled on the pair of wellies by the back door. 'There's no way, no way on earth, my beans'll ever be stringy,' she said.

It was August and the sweet peas were in flower – they take longer to get going in the North. To garden here you need patience. I learned that when I first moved to the farm, *n'er cast a clout til May is out* and all that. Frost was a killer, especially bad for runner beans.

Iris had worked hard all through spring and summer. Now she sat relaxing in an old picnic chair by a folding table. She was wearing jeans and a short-sleeved t-shirt. I sat on the other side of the table in a deck chair twisting the stem of a lavender sweet pea between my thumb and forefinger, putting the flower to my nose.

'That's Camilla, that one,' said Iris.

'Is it? What after *her*? I'm surprised you planted that then. You always said you hated her. I thought, you thought, she was responsible for Diana's death.'

'Well at the time, maybe. Now I don't know. Things happen sometimes beyond our control, fate you know.'

'Yes,' I said, not wanting dissent to waft away the perfume of the day. I never did believe in fate, well not much. I thought, bar major disasters, you made your own luck. I had to think that.

I leaned back in the deckchair and soaked in the sun. The air was filled with the taste of summer: of ripening fruit on canes, tart pink raspberries, green tomatoes, dry earth and rusty water – metallic, like the taste of that first pregnancy. Iris's lighter and cigarettes sat on the table between us, along with a flask of coffee. I wanted to pick up one of her cigarettes, put it to my lips and suck the bitter sweet tobacco down into my lungs, feel the rush in my blood. But I didn't smoke. I'd given up three years ago, when Ronnie nagged me and I didn't have the willpower to resist.

'Take some sweet peas home with you,' said Iris, 'they need picking, make them come that way, the more you pick the more flowers you get.' She smiled, picked up her cigarette packet and turned it over in her hands. She didn't take one out.

'I won't,' I said, 'they'll only go to waste.'

'Why? What do you mean? You off somewhere?

Me, 'Kind of.'

Iris, 'Kind of?'

Me, 'Like you.'

Iris, 'Like me?'

'A place of my own,' I said, 'I need a place of my own. I

can't stay here.'

Iris took a cigarette from the pack slowly and lit up. 'Is it you and Ronnie? What's he done now?'

'Nothing. That's part of the trouble. He's done nothing, we've done nothing. It's like we've given up. We don't talk. He won't. We don't even argue.'

'Well life's better without the arguments, if you ask me. Look at me down to ten a day,' she waved her fag in the air. 'I don't need them now, not like when ...' she stopped.

'Have you heard from Dennis?'

'Never mind him, what about you, you and Ronnie? Is it that bloke you met when you went away with work that time, the architect or whatever he was?'

'No.' I laughed, 'it's not him. It's just... I don't know what it is. I just want something else and what's stopping me? I want to be free like you. Look at you now. Doing what you want, you've got peace and your allotment. You've got the house to yourself, come and go as you please. You even look different.'

'Do I?'

'Never saw you in jeans when Dennis was around.'

'Old fashioned like that he was, said he didn't want other men looking at my arse. I ask you.'

'It's not just the clothes, you look younger – your face I mean.'

'All this fresh air,' said Iris, 'all this digging. You're not going far are you?'

'Back south, I think.'

'Oh.' She sighed, stubbed out her cigarette then lit

another. 'When?'

'Next week for a look round, see about somewhere to live, in a month or two for good. I haven't told Ronnie yet and I've got to hand my notice in.'

'But you've got such a good job at the Library.'

'But it's not enough. It's time I made the break. I'll come back and see you. You can come and see me.'

'It won't be the same.' Iris stood up and moved over to where her runner beans were fast climbing to the top of the canes. She kept her back to me. I watched her tease and readjust her plants. I watched the sun shine through her halo of feathery hair. I watched her become that sparrow chick I'd met for the first time all those years ago. She was right, it would never be the same, and how I was going to live in a place without Iris, without her kitchen and her table and her butter like paste I simply didn't know.

After a while she turned and said, 'I don't blame you. You might meet someone else, they might have bairns, you might get your own ready-made family. Find love where you can. I don't blame you.'

'I don't want a ready-made family. I'm too old for that,' I said pushing the end of my trainer into the hard ground, 'just my own place, like you, have things just as I want: Radio 4 in the morning, candles at night, books and quiet, cheese on toast not stewing steak.'

Iris turned to me, 'it can get lonely *unny*, what about when the dark nights come?'

'It's already lonely.' I said, 'living with someone who doesn't know you're there.'

'But why not here? There's no need to move all that way is there?'

I didn't answer.

'Well, promise me you'll stay in touch. Promise?' I nodded. She came back to the table, twisted the cap off the flask and poured us both a coffee. 'Here's to you then,' she said raising her cup. She reached in her jeans pocket and pulled out a tissue. 'Take some sweet peas anyway.' She blew her nose. 'You're not going for a day or two and I'll see you before you go for good, won't I? Won't I? Grew them for you, you know, runner beans for me, sweet peas for you.'

'I know. Thanks, they're really beautiful. I'll take some,' I said, 'and while we're about it, I think I'll have a cigarette. Just the one,' I said.

'Well you just help yourself *unny*. Do as we please now,' said Iris and she put her head back, looked up at the sky and laughed.

A Bitter Frost

John N Price

It had briefly been a wondrous January sunset, but it was as black as an ashbud now and the frost had already spread its tight embrace. Water was crisping into ice and the coldest air slid down the moorland slopes to settle in the valley. For a moment the distorted branches of a solitary, windswept oak glowed in Elizabeth's headlights as she drove down the steep track to her beloved beckside haven, where a single light sparkled a kind of welcome. People had warned her that winter at the head of the dale would be purgatory but she had loved it. It was the antithesis of her sophisticated workplace and an antidote to the intense busy-ness of the office. She tucked the car into the garage and then drank in the crystal splendours of the evening sky, listening to each ringing star as it revealed itself, every one so much sharper and startling than you could see in a city sky.

She loved winter's spectacular transformations, but she was also fascinated by its grim, cruel power. There was the robin she found frozen solid on her doorstep and the trapped fox hard as iron in the mesh fence at the back of her garden. For a short time each had been beautifully preserved by the phenomenon that had killed it, until the morning's melting. She drank deeply the pure air that smelled of the Arctic and it felt as though she was cleaning out the day's sordid dealings and disputes. It was not the sort of night, however, despite its cold beauty, to be without shelter. She closed the door, hung up her coat and then noticed that the hallway was blue with cold. 'Not again!' she sighed.

Elizabeth turned the thermostat up and climbed the stairs. Her mother was in bed, draped in the old fur coat she had recently unearthed from the depths of her vast wardrobe, her woollen bobble hat perched on her head and a pair of mittens concealing her gnarled, arthritic hands. Her eyes were closed, but Elizabeth suspected she was awake. It was one of her little games. As Elizabeth sat gently on the side of her mother's bed, the old woman gave a startled jump.

'Stop trying to polish me off!' she squealed. 'I'll have a heart attack if you carry on like this.'

'I see you've got your old fur coat on again, mother.'

'It's like an ice box this house.'

'All you have to do if it's cold is turn the thermostat up.'

'Don't know why we had to come and live in this godforsaken dump in the middle of nowhere.'

'You worked the thermostat alright in our old house.'

'I knew where things were there. I was quite happy where we were. I had friends.'

Oh no you weren't happy, thought Elizabeth. Didn't have many friends either. But she said, 'It's a bit early to be in bed, mother. Why don't I rustle up a nice supper and you can come downstairs and we'll watch a bit of telly?'

'Where've you been anyway? It's late and I've had nothing since breakfast.'

'Nothing? Since breakfast? Didn't Debbie give you anything?

'I told her to sling her hook. I don't need a carer. I've got a daughter haven't I?

'Have you really had nothing to eat all day?'

'That's what I said didn't I?'

'And if I ring Debbie she'll tell me the same story, will she?'

'You'd believe her before your own mother wouldn't you?'

'I'll do a meal and when it's ready I'll come and get you and we'll sit together and have a bit of a natter, eh?'

Elizabeth put a lasagne in the oven and took some broccoli from the freezer. She poured a glass of red wine and started to drink it too quickly as she tried to stifle the guilt welling inside her. Yes it had been her decision alone to move to a country retreat, but her mother wasn't exactly in a fit state to participate in decision making about accommodation. Nor had it been just a selfish whim. There were good reasons. It was closer to her new job and the extra money came in handy. There were considerable health benefits for her mother. The clean air for one was beneficial for her COPD. There were lovely walks right from the front door. It was less stressful than city life. God, she thought, I'm starting to sound like an estate agent. She took another slurp of wine. Actually, she had really believed that a change of scenery and a 'fresh start' would improve their relationship which had grown increasingly fraught of late. It hadn't worked so far, though. With mother she felt imprisoned, victimised, even despised.

'Aren't you ready yet?' Mother, standing at the kitchen door. Looking daggers with her piercing blue eyes. She still had her fur coat on, hat and gloves.

'It'll be a while yet. I've only just put it in.'

'Put what in? You're talking gibberish again. It's all the wine. It'll be the death of you. Polish you off it will.'

'I'll have your tea ready in half an hour. You said you hadn't eaten all day.'

'Don't be ridiculous! I've been stuffing myself. I need some exercise now. People eat far too much these days. Look at you. You need to lose two stone. You'd think you were pregnant.' She started to laugh. 'Pregnant! You!'

Elizabeth put down her glass and took her mother by the arm, a little more firmly than necessary. 'Now why don't you just take your coat off and sit down and watch the television until your tea's ready? 'But she knew that it wouldn't work.

'Get your hands off me you upstart you! I'll not be molested by a commoner! Television indeed. I have acquaintances to meet.'

A large anticyclone had settled over Russia and strong easterly winds were blowing in extremely cold air from Siberia. The weather forecasters were predicting it could be the coldest winter since 1947. Elizabeth rang home from her office. Debbie the carer answered. Everything was fine. Elizabeth's mother had had her breakfast and a hot bath and was having her hair done.

'That was your daughter on the phone, Martha. Checking to see if you're alright. Ringing from her office.'

'Checking to see if I've kicked the bucket. Can't wait to get rid of me.'

'She wanted to know if you'd had your breakfast. I said you had and I was doing your hair.'

'I used to go to a proper hairdresser's, a beauty salon in Jesmond. I didn't want to come here you know. We used to live in the city. I had a very lively social life you see. I don't deserve this. Out in the wilds. It's my daughter, she wants to punish me.'

'Punish you? Whatever for?'

'Misdemeanours, minor misdemeanours. Nothing of any significance. But *he* left you know. Went off with some fancy woman to God knows where. Abroad. And she blames me. Says I drove him away and why does she have to be lumbered. Lumbered! You don't expect that from a daughter. Do you know you've got cold hands, Deborah?'

'Oh I'm sorry Martha. Perhaps I should warm 'em up. I hope there's nothing wrong with your central heating.'

'Cold as ice your hands. Everything's cold here. Trying to polish me off.'

'The thermostat's been turned down Martha. That's why it's a bit nippy.'

'The cold kept me awake last night.'

'It was minus ten according to the news.'

'I could feel it in my bones. In my head.'

'Maybe you need an extra blanket.'

'It came in through the window.'

'The window?'

'It stuck its knives into my joints. Sharp, stabbing pains.

Then it went into my brain. It started scuffling around like a, like a... demented rat. So I thought I'm not having this. I haven't come this far to let a bit of cold polish me off. So I gave it what for.'

'You gave it what?'

'I got up, donned my dressing gown, went downstairs and unlocked the door. I went outside and I told it.'

'You told it?'

'Good and proper. About intruding into people's lives. Invasion of privacy. What about *my* Human Rights, I said!'

Oh God, thought Debbie, here she goes again, off into her fantasy world.

When she heard the severe weather warning, Elizabeth told the staff to leave early. She rang home and told Debbie to make her mother comfortable and then make tracks before the roads became too difficult. Then she set off herself, not over-concerned as her four-by-four could cope with severe conditions. Still, she didn't want to leave mother for too long by herself.

Martha looked out of the window at the white wilderness outside. The snow was trying to suffocate her, trying to force its way through the window, blocking the doorways, sneaking down the chimneys. And the house was getting colder. Then the noises started up, the scratching inside her head, rats scrambling to and fro. She started to put her coat and hat on ready for bed.

The frost had formed ghostly fronds on the bedroom window; it started to penetrate the bark of the old oak tree in the garden. It held streams at icepoint, stopped waterfalls in their tracks, froze mammals' breath. Martha lay and listened to its crackling encroachment. 'Godforsaken place this is,' she muttered to herself as she lay, waiting for the attack.

There was a loud crack like a rifle shot as the frost split the trunk of the windswept, tangled oak in the garden and Martha decided she would not be a passive victim. She would confront the enemy on its own territory.

When Elizabeth got out of her car, she paused for breath and wrapped her scarf tightly round her neck. The moon spread a ghostly grey-blue light which was reflected by the virgin snow. The catch on the garden gate was jammed with frost and she had to kick it open. The first thing she saw was the oak tree. Its trunk had been split asunder. It was a cadaver severed by a pathologist's knife, its heart removed. In front of the tree was the outline of her mother with her long fur coat and hat. Elizabeth approached quietly for fear of startling her. The old woman was motionless.

'It's time to come inside mother,' she said gently and put her arm around her shoulders tenderly. But mother did not respond. She was stone cold.

Elizabeth stared into the black, lifeless eyes and saw a reflection of a perfect full moon, crystal clear in the pure air. The beautiful, cold, dead moon. She did not weep but felt a strange satisfaction, a relief, a completion, a heavy burden lifted from her shoulders. And because her mother looked serene, all anger and bitterness dissipated, she decided to leave her there and let the severe frost transfigure her into the noble, dignified and beautiful person she once had been. She gently prised off the gloves and the hat and gave her frozen lips a farewell kiss. And it crossed her mind that after all, maybe this was the reason she'd moved to this godforsaken outpost in the country.

THE GOLDEN VALLEY LINE

Fiona Cooper

I AM ON THE TRAIN FROM SWINDON TO GLOUCESTER, GOING TO MEET my mother. They call this the Golden Valley line and it's a beautiful ride if you've a mind to take it in; which I don't right now.

I was adopted at six weeks, and this will be the first time I've met my mother since then.

I know she's Irish. I know she's a nurse.

I've rushed home from work and changed into the one dress I own, Irish green embroidered with flowers. I've even put on make up, probably badly, after all I never wear make up. If I have a dress style it's sort of hippy/ hell's angel chic, but after all this time I want my mother to think I look good. I've got a bad case of anxious going on like I used to get before exams. The only thing that would stop the seismic tremors was lying on the floor and slowing my heartbeat to just above zombie level, then moonwalking to the exam hall, deaf-mute, on automatic pilot until the damn things were done.

Only you can't just lie down on the floor of a stopping train. I'm sweating and the carriage smells of warm leatherette, cigarette smoke and dust.

She has an Irish lilt, my mother, west country blurred into it, she's lived down here for twenty five years or so.

When I was thirteen, in a rage with my father, I smashed my hand through a glass door and an Irish nurse put thirty three stitches in, talking to me all the time, her voice soothing and mesmerising while my father slid to the floor in a faint. I got a huge crush on her and in the nuclear family ice age where I lived as a teenager, I'd dream about them dying and her adopting me.

Two days after that first phone call, I left a work meeting half way through, couldn't hear anything anyone was saying, and I rang her just to hear her voice again.

She said 'Don't worry, it's alright, it'll be alright, and that.'

I've been reading Flann O'Brian, and the only thing I can remember is a child grovelling in its breech cloth in the ashes. And the phrase *'toshivay, mahogany gas pipe!'* My brain chunters nonsense over and over and now this train's stopped at Kemble, and it'll stop at every station on the way, for God's sake, doesn't anyone know I'm in a hurry? But after all this time, my third cigarette tells me, after all this time, what's the hurry? Patience is a highly overrated virtue, one of the few I've learned to fake over the last twenty two years.

My heartbeat is fast and crazily near my skin, rattling the bones of my chest and fizzing through my head. I want to buttonhole the suit and tie opposite, or grab the lady next to me and gabble, tell him, tell her, tell everyone in this old creaky carriage that I'm going to meet my mother, that I haven't seen her forever, how I've looked for her everywhere, and right now I don't know what to say or think or feel.

For no apparent reason the train brakes scream to a halt, and I look out at the pink gold stone and spring green trees, at sparrows hopping on the ground, starlings sweeping from a tree like rubbish tossed into the air. I see my reflection in the window as smoke gusts by, my hair brushed carefully to fringe over my forehead, my dark straight eyebrows and dark anxious eyes, my mouth set small and straight.

I've seen me a thousand times but this is like a first time and my mouth breathes mist on the glass with a silent HELP. I haven't got a clue who I am right now. I do have a father who was good enough to give to give me his name – *did I ask him? Did I hell, I was six weeks old!* A father who said 'I'll swing for you!' when I wore make up and tried to look smart.

The years of jeers burst into my head like an exploded suitcase, full of stuff you never remember packing and when you see it, you can't imagine why you put it there, what earthly use was any of it and why the hell have you been carrying it all this time?

I don't know what on earth I think I'm doing; after all she gave me away, this mother of mine, and although I know she will have her reasons, I don't want to have to be reasonable any more. My adoptive parents said they wondered if they did the right thing – *we should have had boys!* – after all, my unknown mother had had a baby before me, and the nuns had said there could be Things in my blood. Yeah right, my veins are full of alien corpuscles and I can morph and freeze like a chameleon just to get by.

The train lurches forward, shrieking and creaking and grumbling all the way into Stroud.

Now I'm glad it's a stopping train. Gives me time to try to sort out all this stuff. Stroud looks mellow with golden stone houses perched up the hillside, trees all sunlit and green. The man opposite gets off here, smiling. I'll come back here one day, maybe here will be the place with my place in it, high up on a hill looking over the valley, I could put down roots somewhere like Stroud.

I light a cigarette and slow my heartbeat to zero. The last stop before Gloucester is Stonehouse and I think of John Stonehouse leaving a pile of clothes on a Miami beach and simply vanishing. That's always appealed to me, three times I ran away before I was sixteen, but I always got found, brought back, leathered and even, the last time, forced to wear skirts and dresses. I'm happiest forever in blue jeans.

There's no escape as the train pulls out of Stonehouse, nowhere to get off before Gloucester, well, I could stay on past my stop. Maybe she won't even be there, my elusive mother, maybe I'll just get a coffee and cross back over the bridge and go back.

Hell, this is my last cigarette.

At Gloucester, the platform is crowded but I see her straight away. I think. She's standing absolutely still, wearing the sort of suit that would do for an interview or a low key wedding and she doesn't move an inch as people push past, just scans every face. Then all the people are gone and she is still there and so am I. So it must be her.

We walk towards each other and she takes my hand.

'Oh God dear,' she says, 'I'd know them eyes anywhere.'

And I would too, her eyes and eyebrows are mirrors of mine and she is my height and she says we'll get a coffee so we walk towards the station buffet, I can't believe this is her.

Later someone will tell me *she was a terrible woman, she'd go with anyone, and Drink!* But right now I am drinking her in like cool water in burning sand.

'Well,' she says, 'you've five brothers and sisters at home.'

'You've been busy,' I say, and then I think, oh god, what will she think of me, so I gabble about running out of cigarettes.

In the buffet she gets the coffee and I watch her every move. For all she's small like me, she walks like a duchess, and the serving lady is a grateful minion, and the plastic spoons are heirlooms as my mother picks them up. She sets our tray down as if she owns the place and she's bought me Dunhill Kings, they're the best cigarettes they have. I usually smoke Gauloises but I kind of know Gloucester station buffet won't sell them.

As we talk, she takes my hand and it feels natural, we hold hands on and off between smoke and more coffee.

'I was young,' she says, 'but never a day went past when I didn't think about you. I heard it was schoolteachers that adopted you, and I thought, oh God, if you're a daughter of mine you'll be wild, and they'll be strict.'

'They were,' I say to her question mark eyebrow, 'but it was ok.'

'The thing is,' she says, 'the nuns get you to sign the paper when you don't know what you're doing. Then they send you out shopping – it was a Saturday, and I knew you wouldn't be there when I came back, and you weren't.'

When I was young, my mother told me they'd gone to find a special baby because they couldn't have their own. Told me that she'd picked me up and I'd looked at her and snuggled in and gone to sleep. She'd lined a baby basket with blue satin and when they came to get me, my sister insisted on me being on the back seat of the car next to her. She said that when she held me her heart flipped over and it never flipped back.

'Yes,' says my Irish mother, lighting a cigarette, 'I was out of my mind, you see.'

Later on they'll say *Men? She couldn't be without a man, she'd go with blacks, Egyptians, Chinese, all sorts...* One of my sisters will laugh and say 'She wasn't racist, our Mum, and she was very friendly.'

'What about my father,' I say. On my original birth certificate, he is a dash of faded ink, and she's the only one I can ask after all.

'Oh we were fools,' she says, laughing. 'Young fools. He was in the American air force, you see, and he got called back to America. We laughed all the time, he was hopeless with money and that. One day he took the rent money, and I was beside myself. So he made a pan of fudge and I had to let him off. I was always a fool for fudge.'

I have a million questions, only right now I can't remember any of them. Underneath it all, the only thing that matters is – do you like me? Did you hate me? Might you love me? I'm learning my Irish mother by heart, the way she curls her lip and laughs, her dark wavy hair and every word she says and the way she says it. It never hit me until this moment that I grew up looking like no-one around me. My tall pale serious green-eyed mother, my tall bloodshot hazel father, my brown eyed skinny sister – my aunts and cousins all redhead pale...

And here's my Irish mother, blue eyed, dark browed, my height and build, with a laugh in every phrase.

'Well after that,' she says, 'I got married you see, and when I told him about you, he said we had to find you and bring you home. You'd have been six months old by then. But they told us you'd died. I knew you hadn't, but that's what they told us. The papers were all signed you see. I thought you'd step off that train and knock me to the ground for giving you away.'

'What?' that stunned me, 'I mean, I could have been an abortion... I mean...'

'We don't have abortions in this family,' she says proudly, her chin cutting the air 'There's always room for children. There's had to be.'

She tells me my older sister has the same father as me. That she had four children with her husband and then he was an invalid and she got sterilised after the last one so she had to sleep on the couch for twelve years because he said she wasn't a proper woman. That he had died and she'd had a hard time. More coffee, more smoke.

'You sounded so posh on the phone!' she says, 'And you're training for a teacher? Have you got the look?'

'The look?'

She draws herself up and tightens her mouth to a thin line, raises one eyebrow and turns her eyes to icy steel. I copy every move and she laughs.

'You've got the look,' she says and pats my cheek.

It's strange to feel so warm and relaxed with a stranger – well, a relative stranger. Someone who's my closest real relative and a perfect stranger with it.

'Well,' she says after – good god, four hours?, 'if you're a daughter of mine you'll like a drink?'

'Oh yes,' I say.

'Good,' she says, 'Well I've a fella out in the car so we'll go to Pilton. There's a nice pub there.'

'He's been sitting in the car all this time?' I say as we walk out of the station.

'Oh yes,' she says airily, 'I told him I was meeting you – well, I said you were my niece in case we didn't get on. But now I'll tell him who you are.'

She leans into me as we leave the station and cross the car park. Sure enough, there's a fella sitting in a car smoking with his newspaper propped on the steering wheel and she squeezes my arm. So natural, so warm.

'Bill,' she says, 'this is my daughter, Fiona.'

Bill folds up his paper and smiles at me. He looks like my nice uncle Jack from Devon and when he speaks he has the same accent.

'Pleased to meet you,' he says and grasps my hand. Then he kisses my Irish mother and I get in the back of the car. They glance at each other and smile.

It's an old fashioned pub at the brow of a hill with green valleys as far as I can see. Bill gets the drinks – lager for him, red wine for me and a schooner of sherry for my mother.

She starts feeding the fruit machine and we sit and watch her.

'It'll pay out soon,' he says, 'Cath's only got to touch them machines and out comes the jackpot.'

The way he looks at her she is his jackpot and when she

dumps handfuls of coins on the table like pirate treasure, she gazes at him like he's the end of her rainbow. He scoops up a handful of money and stands up.

'All me winnings!' she says with a note of tragedy,' All you want me for is me fortune!'

He beams and goes to the bar.

'What it is dear,' she tells me, 'I've never had a man like Bill before. When you find love, dear, you grab onto it with both hands and never let it go. I'm glad you found me now I'm with him. There was a few bad years after the husband died. I'm glad you didn't meet me then.'

A shadow crosses her eyes then the curve of her lip flicks it away.

She'd be passed out on the sofa when the truant man came.

Bill brings her two schooners of sherry this time and she laughs as she drains one and starts sipping the next.

'Right then,' she says, and swaggers towards the other fruit machine like a highwayman.

'I've never met anyone like Cath before,' Bill tells me, 'She'll come out with me when I'm working and just stay in the truck till I'm done.'

Cath. My mother. A cascade of coins spills and shimmers round her feet. She sweeps them into her bag.

'That'll do for the chips,' she says, 'Well now, you like to meet your brothers and sisters? It doesn't have to be this time but ...'

'Yeah,' I say, and as Bill drives I sit back and study the curve of my mother's neck and chin and for the first time in forever, I feel like I just might belong.

I wondered what her house would be like. I've lived all over from my detached redbrick childhood through unplumbed basement squats, halfway hippy homes, even a shabby country manor refurbished as a school. I spent one crazy summer stoned in France in a labyrinth of limestone caves bright with rugs from Uzbekistan and shimmering brass lamps smoking from every rough ceiling.

Cath lives in a narrow street of terraces and the hallway is dimly lit, with coats and shoes flung around the staircase. In the sitting room there's a battered couch, a tattered rug, a TV and the walls are patched plaster, frayed paint and peeling paper. *Toshivay mahogany gas pipe!*

'Do you like the wallpaper dear? It's French,' she says, like an eccentric aristocrat deigning to show you her ancestral home.

In the low watt gloom, there's a girl and boy sitting on the couch, the silent TV flickering over their faces. Their eyes glisten and they both smile and we say hi.

'This is Derek and Bridget,' she tells me, 'This is Fiona. We'll have a cuppa. '

The kitchen is a chaos of overloaded shelves, a unit with sagging doors and tired paintwork. Cath steps round the tin bath on the floor and fills the kettle with the aplomb of one who has found the Holy Grail. She lights a cigarette. There's a younger girl in here, tiny faced with huge blue eyes, curled round her knees on one of the mismatched chairs, so quiet and still I don't notice her at first.

'Oh God!' Cath says, 'That one's always hiding, quiet as a

mouse she is, come on Kelly, this is your sister Fiona.'

The little girl smiles and looks at me, looks away, looks again. All the time I'm there I see her watching me, even when we go back in the sitting room, she hangs off the back of the couch. Bill sits in the armchair, Cath beside him, making eyes at him. After a while Bridget and Derek go out of the room and there is only me, Cath, Bill, and Kelly who's slid on the couch beside me, perching like a bird ready to fly.

Cath talks about what she'll do one day when she has her own house. She talks about the three piece suite, the curtains, the carpets, the chandelier and the beautiful big garden with a fountain and fish in a pond. You could be sitting in a nuclear bunker with her and she'd have you tasting the fresh air and smelling spring blossom and admiring the view from the lead-paned windows.

She talks about when her and Bill went to Butlins and were so lovey-dovey that the receptionist thought they were honeymooners.

'I said no,' she laughs. 'We've been married twenty five years and this is the anniversary! Well, that was it. Champagne and roses and a spotlight in the bar – we were proper celebrities weren't we dear?'

Bill's eyes glow with pride and joy.

I talk about the last train back and Cath says no, me and Bill, we'll take you home.

Bridget wants to come but Cath says no. She says it's just a bit of time for me and her. Kelly comes close for a cuddle and her huge eyes meet mine.

'She'll be back,' Cath says.

I will? Oh will I not! My heartbeat and my smile keep pace and I know that nothing could keep me away from my mother's home.

Years later people tell me, *she should never have had fucking kids, she never wanted kids, she walked out on all of them and only came back because their dad was dying.* Years later I'll hear about the drink and the men and the cruelty and the lies and the way she vanished owing thousands.

But right now, Cath, my Irish mother, is getting on the back seat of Bill's car with me. After a while as the street lights fade and there's only the radio and Bill's curling smoke, I lean towards her and she pulls me close, and holds me right into her breasts and I feel so right. Like I belong here, like all the years and the tears and the fears and questions and the doubts and the anger and the not looking like anyone not being like anyone not feeling like anyone just drifts away like morning mist in the first rays of the sun.

SIEVING THE EARTH

Judy Walker

GODFREY WAS MY NEXT DOOR NEIGHBOUR. I WENT ROUND TO INTRODUCE myself when I moved in, told him I had two kids and there might be a bit of noise but he said he was partially deaf, so he probably wouldn't hear them anyway.

I thought he must be about 70. Another neighbour told me he was a widower. His daughter, Eileen, lived not far away. At first I was just aware that he was always out in his garden, digging and hoeing and whatever else it is that you do in gardens. I've never been one for gardening, myself. That was always Kevin's domain so I didn't bother learning about plants and pruning or mowing the lawn. But now Kevin was cutting someone else's grass and I had a new back garden all of my own.

From my kitchen, I could see into Godfrey's garden, so I started to watch him, thinking I might be able to pick up a few tips. When I came down in the mornings to make breakfast at seven thirty, he'd already be out there with his wheelbarrow and spade. I couldn't figure out what he was doing though. He didn't have a lawn like I did – well grassy area would be a more accurate description – just brown earth, like a ploughed field. I thought it must be a vegetable patch but there was nothing in it. Maybe it was the wrong time of year for veg and he was preparing it for the autumn.

I hadn't worked for years so I had no up to date skills but we desperately needed some money to supplement the paltry amount I got from Kevin, so I got a job on the checkouts at Netto. It was boring but there wasn't much stress involved and I got a regular wage and cheap groceries, although the kids pulled faces at the strange brand names I brought home.

When I came in from work each day, Godfrey would still be out there, bending down, digging, raking, heaving stuff into his big old wheelbarrow. Did he spend all day out there? I was intrigued, so one Saturday I made a Victoria sponge and a pot of tea and I took it round on a tray.

'Would you like a bit of cake Godfrey?' I shouted.

He had his back to me, so I walked a bit closer and said it again. He straightened up, like an articulated tent pole being hoisted into position.

'Hello there, Janice.'

'Janet, it's Janet actually,' I murmured. 'I thought you might like a bit of a break. You seem to have been on the go all day.'

'Well, there's always a lot to do.' Godfrey walked stiffly towards the wooden table and chairs on his little patio. 'Have a seat Janice.'

I sat down, poured the tea and cut slices of cake. Godfrey went at the task of eating and drinking in a methodical and concentrated manner. He took a bite of cake, set it down, then sipped his tea, set that down and returned to the cake. It was as though he was taking an exam in afternoon tea consumption and I was the examiner.

'So....what exactly are you doing in your garden, Godfrey?'
I asked at last.

'Preparing the soil.' He looked up at me over his glasses.

'Right, so....?'

Godfrey was a man of few words.

'You'll have to forgive me Godfrey; I don't know anything
about gardening. My husband was always the one that did it
in our family. I could do with a few tips from you, now I'm on
my own.'

'Widowed are you?'

'Er...no. He went off with a policewoman.'

'Ah.'

'So, anyway, you were saying about your garden?'

'If you want to grow anything, you have to make sure the
soil is as good as it can possibly be.'

'Yes.'

'So you don't want anything in it except earth.'

'No.'

'This,' he gestured with a sweep of his arm, 'was all lawn,
but it never grew right. Always had a lot of moss and clover
in it.'

'Oh yes?'

'So, I decided the only thing to do was to dig it all up
and go through every inch of the soil, picking out the stones,
weeds, everything really. If you're going to do a job, you may
as well do it right.'

We sat in silence for a minute or two. I looked more
closely at Godfrey's garden. There were string lines dividing
it up into sections. I asked him what they were for.

'So I know which parts I've sifted. Come with me.' He stood up and, checking I was following, walked back to the section he was working on. He drew on one of his gardening gloves, stooped down and picked up a handful of earth.

'See?' He opened his hand and, with the other, nudged the contents with his horny fingers, revealing a few small stones.

'Mmm,' I said.

He stepped over the string line and scooped up another handful.

'Now, see the difference here.' He tilted his hand and soil drizzled down to the ground, like icing sugar into a cake bowl.

'Oh yes,' I said. 'How do you get it like that then?'

'I've got a sieve.'

I pictured the metal sieve I had hanging on the wall in my kitchen, that I used to drain peas for the kids' tea.

'A sieve?'

'Yes, a soil sieve.' He pointed to a large circular sieve lying beside the wheelbarrow, the sort of thing I imagined gold panners might use.

'So....you're going to sieve all that soil?'

'That's right.'

'It's a big job though Godfrey, isn't it?'

'I've got nothing better to be doing.'

I asked Godfrey if he had any family and he told me he had a son, Will, who lived in Australia and his daughter, Eileen, who visited regularly. I'd never seen her.

'Any grandchildren?' I asked.

'Five – and six great-grandchildren, but I don't see much

of them,' he said. 'Most of them are in Australia. There's only Eileen's two here but they live in London.'

'You don't look old enough for great-grandchildren,' I said.

'I'm eighty-five.'

'Eighty-five? Godfrey, I thought you were about seventy!'

I kept more of an eye on Godfrey after that. I didn't think he should be spending all that time out in the garden. I'd dug over one of my beds and mown the lawn and it had just about killed me. I had blisters on my hand and my back ached for days so I couldn't imagine how he coped, out there every day.

On Saturday mornings I always went to Tesco – I know, busman's holiday. I'd send one of the kids round to see if Godfrey wanted anything fetching and gradually he took to writing me a little list. I carried on taking him tea and cake at weekends as well because it made him have a break. Otherwise I'd see him out there from first thing in the morning till it was getting dark. He never had a day off.

Godfrey introduced me to Eileen one day when she called in to see him. She stayed for an hour on the first Sunday of each month. She'd be about sixty I think, although she looked younger – must run in the family. She had a good figure and her hair was coloured and cut well. I thought she seemed a bit frosty towards me, especially when Godfrey told her I was keeping an eye on him.

'There's no need. I do that,' she said, looking me up and down, taking note of the dark roots coming through in my hair and my Primark trainers.

In the summer holidays the kids used our garden to play

football, which gave me a good excuse not to bother mowing the lawn. The ball regularly got kicked over the fence into Godfrey's. If Eileen was there, she would stare over to our garden and say in a loud voice something like: 'Bloody kids! They should show more respect', but Godfrey never complained. He just threw the ball back or the kids would run round to fetch it. One time when Ross went, he asked Godfrey what he was doing and he stayed and helped him for a bit. Godfrey let him push the barrow.

'Mum, why does Godfrey want all those stones out?' he asked when he came home.

'To make the soil nice, so things'll grow better.'

'Will we have to do that with our soil?'

'Probably not.'

I'd begun to ask Godfrey for advice on what to do with my garden. I told him it had to be low maintenance and I wanted a bit of colour. He suggested a few things, showed me in books and lent me some of his tools.

I got to quite like the feel of the earth with its peculiar combination of hardness and softness – the crust and the cream. I discovered I got a lot of satisfaction from the sticky texture and the loamy smell of freshly turned soil. Sometimes I got a bit carried away and dug down deep, hoping the earth might give up some long buried secret.

Lisa, Ross and I were all round at Godfrey's helping him to sift stones one Sunday when Eileen showed up. She stood watching us, her arms folded. I said should I make us all a nice cup of tea but she said she'd do it and she brought it out on a tray – cup and saucer for herself and mugs for us 'because our hands were dirty'. She talked about how busy she was with her flower club and the council. She was on the parks and cemeteries committee.

'About time you got a bit of colour in here,' she said nodding to the brown earth.

'The soil has to be right first,' said Godfrey, his blunt fingers plucking ineffectually at the silver foil on one of the Kit-Kats Eileen had put out.

'Give it here, Dad.' She snatched it out of his hand and unwrapped it for him.

'Thanks dear. Janice always brings...'

'Janet. It's Janet, Dad,' she corrected.

'I don't mind,' I said.

'Janice was my mother's name.'

'Aah.'

While Godfrey was emptying the wheelbarrow, Eileen said to me: 'You won't get anything from him you know, if that's what you're after. It's all sorted, the will and everything.'

I put in for a supervisor's job at Netto but I didn't get it. Then I saw a job advertised at a garden centre so I applied for that and they took me on. It was a bit better money and I liked the smell of the place – a slightly stale mixture of leaf mould and damp gravel, chemicals, flower scent and sphagnum moss. I learnt the names of the plants we sold and, when I was stacking the shelves, I tried to memorise the information on the boxes of feeder and weeder, Pathclear, potting compost and moss killer.

When I was putting Godfrey's shopping away for him one Saturday I noticed a big chart thing on his kitchen table.

It was a map of our estate with everyone's garden marked on it and a sort of grid thing over them with measurements written along the side.

'What's that, Godfrey?' I asked.

'I was just doing some calculations of how much earth there is to be sifted.'

'I don't think everyone's as bothered about the state of their soil as you are, Godfrey.'

'Well, they should be. It's got to be done.'

'You can't force people.'

'I know – I'm going to do it for them.'

'What? Sift all the earth on the estate?'

'That's my plan.'

'But Godfrey....that'll take......well, years.'

'Good soil is the most important thing in a garden,' he said. He told me that most days. 'Come and look at this.' He took me outside and stooped down to cup a handful of his sieved earth. 'Now, just feel that. That's perfect, that is, like velvet.' He opened his hand out and I pinched the soil between my fingers.

'Wow.'

'You can grow anything in that, Janice. If you get the basics right, everything else will follow.' Godfrey looked at me. 'You understand the earth now, don't you?'

'I do, Godfrey. Yes, I think I do.'

It was lucky it happened on a Saturday, because he could have been there all day otherwise. I was changing the beds upstairs when I heard Lisa shouting to me.

'Come quick. Godfrey's fallen over.'

But it wasn't a fall. It was a heart attack. I wanted to go with him in the ambulance, but they said there was no need, his daughter had been contacted.

They all turned up for the funeral – Eileen and her family and Will and his lot even came over from Australia. They sat there in the front pews, sniffing and dangling hankies. I stayed near the back. I was sad it wasn't a burial because I felt sure that's what Godfrey would have wanted – to be down there in the earth, feeding the soil. I didn't go to the crem – that was family only.

For weeks afterwards Eileen was at Godfrey's house every day – clearing it all out I suppose. She barely spoke to me, just a few words to let me know they were putting it up for sale.

'I told you that you were wasting your time if you thought you were going to get anything from my father,' she said.

'Your dad gave me the earth,' I said, looking her straight in the eye.

'What? What do you mean by that?' Her tone was sharp. Then she realised what I meant. 'We're having the garden turfed over. Nobody would ever buy it the way it is – all that horrible brown mud.'

'But God...your dad spent so much time-'

'He was going quite senile, of course.' She tapped her head.

I waited till she'd gone and then I went round to Godfrey's. I hadn't told Eileen that I still had a key. The house was cold and echoey and I felt uncomfortable being there. It was a long shot but I had to try. Not on the hall table, nor the kitchen...the living room – I scanned it from the doorway. Yes! Beside the fireplace stood a large brown plastic jar with a label fastened to it by a thick rubber band.

Outside, dusk was falling and the shapes in Godfrey's garden were blurring at the edges. I could just make out the shape of the soil sieve, propped up against the shed wall. I took it and walked to the middle of the garden, unscrewed the jar and shook the contents onto the sieve. Then I scattered them over the earth and I raked the soil over and over and over, till it was like velvet.

WAITING

Beda Higgins

BEARDED FRAN SAT ASTRIDE HER STOOL PEELING WAXY POTATOES. Her reedy arms swung from her squat body. She looked across the sky, watching a red evening roll in. She was waiting for her cowboy to ride across the horizon. He'd love her fuzzy smallness, and he'd stroke her hairy back. She'd be ten feet tall.

'Day dreaming again eh Fran?' said Ringo passing her caravan.

She grinned. 'One day it'll come true.'

He laughed. 'And I'll win the lottery.'

Fran didn't care for money. It wouldn't make her taller, or less hairy. She dreamt of love, absolute head over heels love. She knew it'd happen one day. Gypsy Rosa had seen it in her tea leaves.

She saw him coming out of the big top and her heart galloped, she couldn't take her eyes off him. She wondered what was wrong with him. Everyone that worked at the circus had something wrong with them. She scrutinised his walk – no limp or unusual gait. His brown weathered face had no lumps or bumps, he looked healthy even. He wore an open neck checked shirt and denim trousers. His eyes were very blue.

He passed her caravan, and nodded, 'morning.'

She grinned and giggled, giddy with anticipation.

Over lunch Ringo told the rest of the circus troupe, 'he said he was a mature student finishing off his studies and had a bit of spare time on his hands. He said he wanted to do something practical and short term, to give his brain a rest.'

'Another bleedin' dreamer then,' said Tania, one of the acrobats.

Ringo sniffed, 'well he's not our concern. He doesn't have much to offer, and we're not short of staff at the minute.'

Fran bit her lip, it only took one accident and they would be short staffed.

The next day Joe got stomach ache so bad he had to go to hospital.

'Terrible state he's in, they've put one of those drips in him because he can't keep anything down,' said Ringo.

'I reckon it was the cockles he had at Morecambe,' said Myra.

Fran listened and smiled. 'There'll be work for someone then.'

'Aye, I'll give that bloke a ring.'

She nodded. Joe needed to lose a few pounds.

The man jumped out of the van the next day and waved the driver off. He had high cheekbones and strong features. Fran liked that. She watched him from a distance. Maybe he was one of those getting away from the rat race. The circus had had them before, the ones who couldn't face another day. They usually shacked up in a caravan and tagged on for a week or two, mucking the cages out. Then they got sick of greasy food and went back to where they came from. Some of the drifters were grieving – they'd lost children to drugs, or were recently divorced. They didn't realise grief travels with you. They never lasted long. The worst were the rich indulged students who'd 'dropped out.' Those long limbed, healthy, smooth skinned creatures that moaned '*I don't feel I belong anywhere.*'

'Feckless' Fran muttered. She wouldn't give that sort the time of day. She spat, 'not anymore.' They never took any notice of her, she was invisible to them. She wasn't anything special, not like the acrobats or the lion tamer or the clowns. She was just the deformed bearded lady, who also happened to be a dwarf.

She could see the new man was different. Perhaps he'd had a breakdown, but there were none of the lingering wounds. No nervous tic, no hand wringing, no looking down at his shoes. He walked purposefully, a man who knew what he was doing.

'He's going to paint the wagons and all the woodwork in the big top, proper handyman he is,' said Myra the snake charmer with a greedy glint in her eyes.

He liked Fran's coffee. She gave him a mug at breakfast, one at twelve and one at four. He was quiet, she liked the quiet sort. He nodded putting his empty coffee mug down and his blue eyes shone, 'thanks.'

Myra and Fran sat in the launderette watching the glittery acrobatic frocks go round and round. Myra looked at Fran, 'you're smitten aren't you?' she teased.

Fran felt her blood surge, she pushed her pinched small

face up close, 'mind your own business Myra, I'm warning you.' Fran had never been in love before, she sat back trembling. This was it, her cowboy in the sunset she'd been waiting for.

Myra looked at her nails, 'he'll be off Fran. Drifters, they're no good. He'll break your heart, I can tell. He's not interested in a relationship. I think he might be gay.'

Fran turned on her, 'did he refuse your offer of a few acrobatic flips eh?'

'Oooohh, who's got it bad,' Myra sniffed.

Fran thought he might be a priest who'd lost his vocation. He had a soulful, thoughtful look about him. *Wistful that's what he is*, she smiled to herself. Sometimes, when Fran handed his coffee over their hands touched round the mug. She wouldn't wash her hand all day to keep a bit of him on her.

She knew he wrote every night in his caravan, she'd spied on him tip tapping on his computer. She imagined poetry and songs. Perhaps he'd sing to her one day.

She made him fairy cakes to go with his coffee, and offered to do his washing for him.

'It's all right Fran thanks, I can manage, but we can chat a while if you like. Tell me about yourself.'

Fran had stayed awake at night trying to prepare her answer to this. If they were going to get married they needed to know about each other. She thought she might say 'I was abducted at birth from a wealthy family.' Or maybe something more dramatic, 'I have gypsy blood in me, from a clan with magical gifts' and she'd stare mistily across the horizon.

But when he asked she wanted to tell the truth, because that's how they'd be, honest and truthful with one another throughout their lives. 'I've always lived in a circus,' she told him. 'My Mother was a bearded dwarf and my Dad was one of the acrobats. I wasn't close to either of them. They made me feel as if I was a burden – just another mouth to feed. They both died in a circus fire five years ago. It was a relief to be honest.'

'Fran, I'm sorry,' he said.

She knew he meant it.

'Did you go to school?' He asked.

'No, no need for that in a circus, and we move around. It's not nice to always be the new one, especially if you're a bit different.'

'So did you get any education?'

'I've learnt everything there is to know about life from working at the circus. I know there are good folk and there are bad. I'm better here than out there. You could say I've a degree in human nature.'

He smiled, 'I'm sure you have. What about friends, did you have anyone to play with?'

'Sometimes seasonal workers would bring their kids and I'd play with them, but they never stayed long. I always had the animals to play with. Nelly is the same age as me. She thinks she's my twin sister by the way she trumpets every time she sees me.'

He smiled again. 'You're very sweet natured Fran.'

She put her head to one side, 'can I show you something?'

'Okay.'

She led him to a small tent next to the big top. In it were mirrors, lots of fairground mirrors. Different distorted images stared back; fat and thin, little and large.

'Stand here,' she said. She stood in front of a mirror next to his. In his reflection he was squashed small and fat, his face was a troll's grimace. In her mirror she was elongated, her short limbs were lengthened and stretched. Her round pug face seemed sculptured, her dumpy figure shapely and slim. She pirouetted slowly in the mirror, watching her elegant reflection. 'Now tell me, do you feel any different even though you look different?' she asked him.

'No.'

'Well neither do I. Look at me in the mirror. I'm the same inside as other women, I have the same desires.' She tried to lock his blue eyes with hers but he looked away mumbling, 'I'm sure you do Fran '

She liked the way he whistled quietly as he painted. He was neat and tidy, always cleaned up after himself and put the brushes away. Too soon he finished the paintwork and Joe came back. Joe was pale, but willing and able. There was no extra work for the man.

'Sorry mate, I'll have to let you go,' said Ringo.

'No problem, it's been good, thanks.'

'Would you paint my caravan before you go?' Fran asked coyly, 'I can pay you.' She'd emptied out her life savings and counted it all the night before.

He shrugged, 'a couple more days won't make much difference. We can have our last little chat eh?'

She wanted him to see how tidy and neat her caravan

was. He'd realise then what a good wife she'd make. He could move into her caravan and work at the circus. Ringo liked keeping it in the family; that's what he'd be once they married. If he didn't want to roam round the country with the circus she'd even live in one place with him. A cottage would be nice, somewhere remote. They'd live off the land. At night he'd read to her, their life would be pure and simple. She knew it was what he was looking for.

She baked shortbread.

'Yummm, I love shortbread,' he said taking another piece with his coffee.

'Me too,' she smiled. 'Isn't it funny how much we've got in common?'

'What do you mean Fran?'

'Well we both like shortbread, and we like each other's company, and we like the simple life. All we need is the here and now and each...'

She didn't finish her sentence. He was looking at her, eyebrow raised as if at that moment something clicked.

Yes that's right, we are deeply in love. She smiled, *what a sweetheart, it's only just dawned on him.*

'I'd better be off Fran.' He put his cup down quickly. He didn't look at her as he left.

She sat down and wrote a list of who she'd invite to the wedding. She'd invite the whole circus troupe, even Myra. The trapeze twins could be her bridesmaids. Then she wrote a list of wedding presents. She fell asleep mulling over what she should wear for her honeymoon.

The next morning it was a bright, blue day. He knocked

on her door. 'I was wondering if you fancied a little walk Fran?'

'Why yes, I'd love one.' She grabbed her cardigan and stepped out of the caravan. He held her hand coming down the steps and offered his arm to her. They headed down towards the river. Fran felt dizzy, *he's realised he can't fight it. He's going to propose by the river surrounded by wild flowers and birds singing and the rush of bubbling water.*

He didn't say anything while they were walking, Fran understood, *he's trying to get the words right in his head.* They stepped into a bluebell-carpeted wood. It was shaded and cool.

He cleared his throat, 'I want to thank you very much for everything Fran. You've made me feel welcome.'

'My pleasure,' she nodded demurely.

'I'm leaving tomorrow. I need to get my thesis handed in.'

Her heart raced, 'tomorrow?' She'd already decided that when he asked, 'will you come with me' she'd go; – *but tomorrow? It'll hardly give me time to pack.*

'What's a thesis?' she spluttered trying to give herself time to get her thoughts in order. *I'll have to break it to him gently that I need at least a week to pack up.*

'A thesis is an academic book. Mine is about travellers. I've been observing and writing up how they live all round the country.' He looked at her, 'your circus was the last part of the project. I've tried to integrate with each group, living in their community for a short time. I've got all the information I need now, and I'll go back home and write it up. My wife's probably forgotten what I look like.' He laughed gently.

'Your wife?'

'Yes, I have a wife.' He turned to her, 'Fran our little chats have been particularly helpful – thank you.'

He has a wife. 'Why?' she stamped the ground.

'What do you mean?'

'Why have you tricked us?'

'It's much better if subjects don't know they're being observed. That way I can get a truer more objective grasp of your lives. I don't think any harm's been done.'

Fran clenched her fists, 'how we live is no-one's business but ours.'

'It's interesting historically and as a social commentary.'

She thought of all the things she'd told him. Hands on hips she stepped toward him, 'I don't want you to write about me. It's bad enough that people gawp at me day in day out, without them gawping into my life in a book.' She stomped her little fat legs, 'Never! You are not allowed. You pretended to love me and all the time it was trickery to get your story.'

'Fran' he said gently. 'I never once exploited you or gave you reason to believe I loved you.'

Fran's eyes narrowed, she jabbed a shaking finger at him, 'you're wicked. You'll get your come-uppance. I'll make sure you do, you'll be sorry, and...' red faced unable to contain her fury, she threw her head back and howled.

He stepped away, 'I'm sorry that's the way you feel Fran. I'm sorry I'm leaving on a sour note. No one will know it's you, you won't be named and...

She spat in his face.

He wiped his eye, 'I better go.'

Myra knocked on Fran's caravan that evening after the show. 'We're all having a few drink at my place, d 'you want to come over?'

'No thanks Myra.'

Myra shrugged, 'please yourself.'

It was a beautiful summer evening, still and calm. The circus had great takings all week because of the glorious weather. Fran sat on her stool. The laughter from Myra's caravan drifted on a warm breeze. She stared across the orange and red horizon, – the same colours the sky had been the night her parents died. She sniffed the whispering summer air, her skin prickled goose flesh remembering it all.

Fran couldn't sleep and stared up at a star-filled sky. Later, she watched giggling silhouettes stagger away from Myra's. They fumbled into their caravans to sleep heavily.

They were roughly woken by the crack and cackle of flames in the early hours of the morning. The befuddled circus troupe lurched from their bunks and ran for their lives.

At the inquest it was stated the man had rigged up some dodgy electrical wiring so he could use his computer in the caravan. It was an accident waiting to happen. The circus was exonerated from any blame.

The next site was on soft green pastures on the outskirts of the town. Fran carried her wash-bag between the caravans. She looked across the horizon and knew one day her cowboy would come riding home. She smiled to herself, 'and when he does, I'll be ten feet tall.'

The Remainder

Amanda Baker

Worrying a hangnail, she snagged loose skin on the side of her thumb. The self-heal implant kicked in, releasing smart drugs to her nervous system. It was a big overreaction but the same would happen if she ruptured her spleen or broke a bone. Given that she was personality type B2Z, this was unlikely. Laura twisted her hands together, her gaze fixed on the monitor.

Laura was a throwback, classified with a handful of others who displayed genetically remembered emotions and chemical instability echoes from the last of the Naturals. She was not one of those but suffered inconvenient similarities and submitted without complaint to supervision. As a younger woman she'd been studied intermittently. They had plenty of data on her type. Those carrying out the research asked three non-essential questions in any half hour period as they had been taught. As part of the unspoken bargain, she practised suppressing inappropriate impulses. Keeping the diary had been their idea; she could not see the point. Laura intended to Delete All when she got her ICN – Imminent Cessation Notification.

Twenty seconds later, Laura put her finger back to her mouth; there was no frayed skin. Nevertheless it was a habit she could not kick.

(entry 207)
News today of Kay Adams – 163-year-old mother – who survived eight types of cancer, inexplicably succumbed to natural death. The world population or 'The Remainder' now stands at 7,472,930. For fourteen months The Remainder had stayed at 7,472,931. That '1' was an absurd comfort to me. I obsessed about the '1' and was reprimanded – kindly – for inducing a problematic emotion. But we, The Remainder, identified with it the way we could not with the other seven million plus. My imagination is the bane of my life. I thought of the '1', the actual figure, as a some-1. And there she is. I can't look away. Kay as a child in the 1980s in a grass garden, wearing a dress made of real cotton. I ache to touch the material and smell the greenery. Then there's Kay at college, Kay at work, Kay aged fifty-two with her first baby and so on. Word Picture News cleared as I blinked. I'm fed up of Kay Adams. I dislike back-looking, or future-looking for that matter. If you can't be old until you're 140 I'm only middle aged. Middle of what? I've no sense of beginning or end. I've been diagnosed with Time Fear, the latest and most common, potentially psychotic sickness. Though I am only waiting for the same thing as everyone else, I cannot clear the agitation. I feel sick dread, painfully edged with hope. It ambushes me. I can't settle.

(entry 209)

When the intercom buzzed today, followed by the caller recognition indicator, 'Neighbour – Sarah – casual call – one hour – no refreshments required,' I allowed the pre-set to run. 'Occupant – Laura – unavailable due to requested sleep extension.' There is no boredom option. I dislike myself. Oppressive guilt is something else I could do without. A companion left me recently despite over ninety percent match testing. I would leave me if I could. I've worked through every conversation with every occupant of the thirty-seven units in this block. It would have been more considerate to display, 'unit unoccupied' but everyone knows there's no insect clearance for outside. Clearance has been promised repeatedly for nearly three weeks. Uselessly I punched the information pad with the same question. The insecticide units were working overtime to produce enough effective drop-chems.

Again I press my forehead hard against the wall. Marginally cooler than the ambient temperature of the air, it gives short-lived relief. Should I try an individual cell? Some are still habitable. It's twenty years since I last lived that way; the cold was unbearable at night. There were unsettling noises all the time. Ultimately the desired solitude made one anxious. There was no security. From what? I don't really know, but it felt unsafe. There's only reliable energy for the large multi-occ units now. I don't really mind.

(entry 220)

I lie on the day-pad to escape the heaviness. Heaviness – that's the only way to describe it. If I did not know better I'd say the air pressure in my cell is wrong. I struggle to breathe although the pressure gauges have been stable for months.

The music tones do not lift me. The gentle vibration of the rest-pad irritates me like a snoring lover; it's out of rhythm with some internal setting and the aroma of artificial lavender makes me nauseous and sad. It's nothing like the lavender pillow grandmother gave me in 2083, whatever the rep says. Granny paid a week's living allowance for the dried flower heads on the black market and made pillows for me and my cousin Zane. We were spellbound by her stories of grass gardens and snow and rivers and shopping. Zane had wanted to dissect the lifestyle, calculate how one shared space in a disorganised environment, but I just wanted to *be* them. Zane and I sometimes pretended to be siblings but usually we could only communicate by micro-mail. There were limited opportunities to replicate the situations painted in such detail: collective meals, arguments, making up, hiding in a house that belonged just to one family, sharing or fighting over toys. I couldn't grasp it, neither could Zane but I cried for it.

(note)

I was told my jealousy was irrational when it was announced, early in 2098, that my cousin was pregnant. I was pressed into counselling. Mandatory medication was ordered when I lurched into depression after Zane's baby died. The little boy was born with Zero Life Will, a non-biological, non-genetic, non-chemical syndrome and therefore incurable. Initially it had been feared that the condition might be contagious. Some argued that it was, but only psychosomatically. All forms of psychosomatism are curable too with smart bio-chemicals. The specialist did agree that the jealousy and sadness had the same source – another worrying statistic.

That year, forty-eight babies were born worldwide. Ten lived normally, twenty-two underwent bio and/or genetic reconstruction and sixteen were born with Zero Life Will. Of the thirty-two live babies, only six girls and two boys had FRP, Functioning Reproductive Potential. The ZLW babies remained a medical and scientific conundrum. Their little corpses were studied extensively but the ZLW body parts were never used for transplant or other medical applications. They never worked.

Zane was unable to have a death ceremony for her baby until four years later, by which time there were two crates of secondary body tissue along with the tiny butchered original. When the ZLW babies were a new phenomenon, artificial organs were transplanted into them and they were kept on high-intensity, multi-function life sustainers but the organs never worked independently once inside these infants. A scientist, who had exhaustively studied ZLW, proclaimed after years of study, that the babies simply did not want to live. He was hounded out of the World Fertility Council. I can't recall his name.

(entry 223)

I hoped the false lavender would trigger a sensory memory of the real thing but it's too long ago. The small pouch containing the precious flower-remains had been made of cotton, like Kay Adam's dress. The material disintegrated even though I tried not to handle it. During the great plagues of 2103 when a cloying, fetid stench fouled the air for months, I forced my precious lavender pouch to my nose even though there was only the faintest trace of its aroma. I tried breathing through it, ignoring the muggy brown air which was like my own fear. In those days the air was always adulterated with some chemical or other. Every year the food developers created new seeds to keep ahead of the mutated crop diseases. I vaguely remember a seven-year cycle. But eventually the developers found they were only two seasons away from earth zero. That was when the super-plagues arrived. Also the nightmares that I still have. Millions were already weakened from unwholesome synthetic nutrition. It was in 2103 that we took our biggest hit. Food supplements could not prevent starvation, even in the Priority Nations. The Sub Nations ceased. I can hardly visualise a Sub Nation now. They are a shameful footnote; areas bombed for their oils and natural resources by coalitions controlling the peace weapons. Even in grandmother's time it was accepted that there was little practical purpose in shoring up the fragile populations of countries that, in the pre-plague years, failed to hand over resources to the Democratic Council of Nations. We were taught at school that areas of the globe historically suffered from famine and various economic and geographical crises. There was an unspoken understanding that it was the natural order of things that these branches of the human tree be allowed to wither for the benefit of The Remainder. Lots of things are unspoken now. These are the things that hurt my head. The 'natural order of things' isn't much used as an argument the rest of the time.

(note)
Untagged genetic engineering led to plant and human infertility. Allied with the fashion prevalent in the mid 2000s of delaying parenthood until the mid fifties, The Remainder plummeted to unsustainable levels.

(entry 225)
For no reason, I've been thinking of Rory. Do I miss him or am I bored? How can you know? We met through cycling. Having a common interest is important but when we were alone, things became odd. I wanted him here but his presence irritated me. Maybe there was just no *point* to it. We had sex, obviously, but it became an absurd activity to me. Neither of us had the means to reproduce and if one wants body-pleasure, there are so many other less messy ways... In the end it was sensible Rory who pointed out that we'd only achieved seventy percent match test. It was a kind, tactful way of ending things. I don't know why I thought of him.

(note)
Precautions were put in place governing the use of pleasure chemical stimulators and simulators. Prior to metabolic

monitoring, there were deaths from excess. Users forgot to eat or exercise. Everyone is lectured on the use of self-gratification equipment. Knowing it's there whenever you wanted it with little effort, eventually diminished interest and there are few accidents from overuse these days.

(entry 226)
I'm trying to find out how my grandparents met and became a couple without using match testing but that sort of information is not available on the family history files. I can't picture them as young people. I know they lived together in a house. They had two children at a very early age, just in their mid forties. Their daughter Jade, my mother, was kept alive artificially for seven years because extensive and invasive treatment ruined her body. My mother (the woman who grew me), was treated with a cocktail of drugs, genetic modifiers and hormone stimulators to prevent rejection of a transplanted womb. The womb had been removed from a twelve-year-old girl who'd never animated but was kept on artificial support until her organs were ripe because she was found, during the routine birth check, to have Functioning Reproductive Potential. The non-animated donor's name was Laura.

(note)
Many methods were tried. Cloning was one of the ugliest disasters. Clones never had FRP. The ones that survived for any length of time were prone to self-destruct and there were a number of highly publicised cases of Clones deliberately

causing death in others. Clone rampages filled us with terror. The age of consent for sex was lowered; couples were encouraged to have natural sex and not use contraception. After a while contraception was outlawed. Intrusive genetic screening prior to reproduction became mandatory. Any matched couples found to be genetically compatible were required to have natural sex. They also had to agree to split samples, which could be implanted into women who had functioning wombs but could not conceive. Growing babies entirely outside the human body had been tried also, but like the clones these creations were unacceptable.

(entry 228)
Level three insect clearance has been announced. Most people won't go out at level three but I'm desperate. I managed the celloplate covering without claustrophobia this time, processed my body through the biowave chamber and was foam-sprayed in the outer cubicle. The electronic aunty asked if I was sure I wanted to go out and was I aware that it was only level-three clearance? I know the tone to use and answered yes, firmly, to both questions. There was a cursory mental health grade query before I was allowed to leave the building.

Even though I breathed carefully through the nylon visor I nearly choked. The rubber taste of chemicals spread over my tongue into my throat. I lowered my breathing and tried not to glance down. It's hard to ignore the crunching under foot. Away from the building, the path was clearer. The only other vehicles out were the gigantic vacuum trucks.

There was nowhere I wanted to go; I just needed to be out of the cell. Cycling past a deserted outdoor recreation area, I noticed it'd been re-painted. It's a weird colour. They must be running out of green.

(note)

No germination is allowed outside the huge seed factory farms for fear of uncontrolled mutation contaminating the precious grain-grow sites. Patches of earth are ventilated, overlaid with netting and watered to reduce dust storms, but cleared of vegetation. Old style concrete and other covering materials are kept to a minimum because of flooding.

(entry 230)

Today, without intending to, I cycled to an indoor recreation unit I'd not visited for months. It made my outing seem less aimless. They had a screen of course. There were only a handful of people inside, we didn't acknowledge each other. It was as if there was a collective agreement to underplay the situation.

I recognised most of those in the rec, but two were new. People seldom travel without a work reason. There were two men, one about my age, the other nearing retirement, about 105 I think. They sat by the counter with drinks. The fair-haired man was obviously the result of the genetic choice programme before it was restricted. He had enormous blue eyes that sagged uncomfortably at the sides and he was so tall that a titanate back frame supported him. The man by his side was about average height, 6ft 4 and although wearing a lung capacitor, he seemed healthy and rather good-looking. I had to force myself not to stare at him. When I got out from the third inner chamber, leaving the suit in the second, as required, I glanced over without hindrance of screens or visor in what I hoped was a casual manner. The man with the lung capacitor was looking at me. Fortunately there wasn't time for self-consciousness. I smiled and made sure I got a seat where I could see him.

I was about to order hot Soya, having gone through the pretence that there was anything else, when Word Picture News announced that Elayne Rhonan, who had gone into natural labour six hours earlier, was about to give birth. This was it at last. Silence descended on the bar. Someone coughed, ordinarily a matter of interest. On this occasion no one paid any attention.

After a short commentary by the lead doctor, the screen blanked for a moment. Then we were shown inside a large white room where a dozen medical staff surrounded by monitors, life sustainers and other standard equipment hovered at their stations. In the centre on a waist high surgical pallet was a young woman in a green gown. A doctor at the woman's left shoulder was listening to electric pulses and telling her when to push. I struggled to breathe. I've seen demonstrations of real birth but never as it happens. All The Remainder would be watching and waiting but this felt as if it was about me.

(note)

It had been agreed by the Fertility Council that, after recent disasters, there would be only necessary interference, whatever that meant. The pregnancy was fully monitored and Elayne had not been allowed to leave the hospital since conception was confirmed. The mother-to-be was fed on a special diet of non-modified foods, accessed by top Fertility Council officials from a dwindling and secret source.

(entry 230 continued)

The pregnancy has progressed well. Everyone had access to the scans. I know lots of people have printouts on their cell walls but I have a good quality one, which cost extra, by the side of my rest unit. Even on the scratched public screen you could tell that Elayne was extremely young. She had been forty four when she'd conceived and had just had her forty-fifth birthday.

After almost fifteen excruciatingly long minutes, during which time my Soya drink went cold and got scummy, it was announced that the baby's head was crowning. One of the doctors examining Elayne gestured. The second doctor called for equipment and a nurse standing behind her handed over what looked like small shears. Even though I know that Elayne had total pain-block, I crossed my legs. A nervous young medic, who in his seventy-six years had only minimal experience of physical medicine and had never seen a natural birth, fainted and was spirited away which reminded me to breathe properly. There was nervous laughter in the bar and then quiet again. It was announced that the baby's head was out. Shortly afterwards, the slimy grey/blue cord was severed and the whole infant was carefully lifted and placed into an incubator.

Attention switched immediately from Elayne to the baby. There was a camera lens in the crib next to the life monitor. I've never seen a newborn child. I got a powerful ache in my chest; my abdominal muscles contracted and for the first time since Rory left, the back of my throat tightened up and my eyes watered. The child seemed in some ways featureless although it had dark hair. I wonder if Zane's baby had resembled this scrunched red bundle. A nurse wiped the animated child with surgical cloth. It was a much messier business than I'd imagined. They tried to attach the monitors for the birth check but it was slippery. One nurse dropped a circulation monitor and was dismissed. The child had a scummy covering on its skin and disproportionately large fists but I've never seen anything so beautiful. Then it started to howl. A woman in the bar complained vehemently that the child was distressed and they should leave it alone. An older man said that he had heard that all babies cried and it was nothing to worry about. I don't know who was right. An almost passionate disagreement erupted in the bar. I glanced across to the man with the lung capacitor. He smiled at me, a friendly pleasant smile. Maybe it was the shock of the moment and the excitement of the birth report but I felt something like a dull electric throb in my belly. I would talk to him. The live report shut down temporarily. They were receiving complaints about the crying. It was announced that they would recommence broadcasting as soon as all the checks were complete.

I ordered more Soya for something to do and scanned the weather reports on the table-screen. The man with the lung capacitor was staring at me and I wished I'd used a mirror before rushing out. It's rare that you meet new people. Everyone was impatient for the report to recommence and complained to the barman as if he could do anything about it. Suddenly the screen beamed again. One of the medical team who had been in the background during the birth was holding the new baby, now clean and quiet. Everyone in the bar stared. I stared, hoping that we'd be able to download pictures. The man announced that it was a girl. There was a huge cheer in the bar. She was going to be called Hannah. Some approved the name and some did not but it was a new thing to discuss. I like the name. Her weight was declared as was her length, bone density, projected intelligence, eye colour etc. I was transfixed by the cross-looking infant and thought again how incredibly beautiful she was. The child's mother was going to look after her with the help of a team from the fertility unit. I knew from my old counselling that the spiky sickness I felt then was jealousy. Elayne would need further medical input to recover from the birth and detox from the drugs. That wasn't the news we were waiting for.

As if someone had flicked a switch I thought about my mother. Not as the woman I did not resemble, encased in a square picture slot on the wall, but the person who'd given birth to me. I wondered what it would feel like to have a belly distended enough to carry another human being. Would walking be uncomfortable? Did it get in the way? For a while I dreamed the old daydream, the one where I ambled along with a tiny person tottering beside me. The child looks like me, only she is small. The dream ends, as usual, unsatisfactorily because the child does not seem childlike but simply a miniature adult. I cannot pin down what it is about children that makes them children and the dream breaks.

It seemed that the broadcast would end without answering the most important question but then the screen moved to a well-known presenter. A small picture of Hannah remained in the right hand corner. I watched the miniature picture as the baby scrunched its fists and did a big yawn with its tiny mouth. The presenter announced that whilst Hannah was normal, it had been confirmed that she had been born with no trace of FRP. The hush in the bar reduced to a vacuum of sound. Someone blanked the screen. I felt wobbly. Too much emotion after extended confinement I expect. Two women who had been arguing energetically left in silence. I stared down at the steaming Soya. I knew I'd throw up if I touched it. I was aware that the man with the lung capacitor said something to his friend and they stood up to leave. As they drew level with my table the younger man slowed. I thought about looking up and making eye contact but I didn't. The men kept walking. I cycled home.

Daft John

Rosemary Brydon

ELLEN COULD SEE MR REID'S OUTLINE THROUGH THE GLASS IN HIS office door. She sat up straighter on the hard leather chair. Mr Reid's secretary, Miss Morris, looked up from the typewriter keys, which her fingers were striking quickly and rhythmically.

'I'm sure he won't be much longer,' she said.

'It's not a problem,' Ellen said. 'I'm not in any hurry.'

The precise tapping resumed, accompanied by regular little pings at the end of each line. The gas fire in the narrow black-leaded iron fireplace hissed and sputtered almost in time. The opaque glass in the bottom half of the window behind Miss Morris was a perfect match for the cold grey sky in the clear top half. It was such a dull day the gaslight in its pale green globe was already lit. At first glance there wasn't much here to suggest that Mr Reid was one of the wealthiest landlords on Tyneside, Ellen reflected: there was a second chair alongside the one she was sitting on, a large faded print of an Egyptian temple in a wooden frame above the fireplace, and a tall glass-fronted bookcase by the door inside which several large ledgers leaned crookedly against each other. Miss Morris' desk took up most of the rest of the space; the strip of matting under her feet was the only concession to comfort. An indented and scuffed track crossed the floor in front of her desk from the outside door to the inner sanctum.

But although the office was functional and unostentatious, the furniture was best quality mahogany and leather, and the flooring was the highest grade cork linoleum, buffed to a reflective sheen with lavender-scented floor polish. Miss Morris was more than satisfied with her surroundings and conditions of service; she had worked for the Reids, father and son, for over twenty years. The office was an indicator of Mr Reid's standards; he cared for his properties and the people who lived and worked in them. He employed rent collectors but still liked to visit his tenants himself, and he was always sure of a welcome and a cup of tea whenever he chose to call.

'I'm sorry Ellen, but I have nothing to suit you at the moment,' Mr Reid said, straightening up from the ledger he had been checking. 'If anything comes up I'll let you know.'

'It's a pity,' Ellen said. 'I just called on the off chance, you know. We manage well enough I suppose, but with the girls being grown up and the three boys, we could do with more space than two bedrooms. The girls have a Dess bed* in the living room and the youngest has a truckle bed in our room, but it's far from ideal. And we can afford something better now that the girls are working.'

'Is Will still at the steel works?' Mr Reid asked.

'Yes. He's a special slinger.'

'That's a dangerous job isn't it?'

'Yes. He guides the cauldron over the shop floor. That's another reason why I'd like something bigger. He works hard

Fold up bed

and we're all on top of each other in the house. There's no peace.'

'Have you thought of an exchange?'

'I have; but who would want to move into a smaller house?'

'Well, I have one possibility on my books, old John Pattinson. Perhaps you know him? He's quite a local character; some people call him Daft John. But that shouldn't matter, you'd be just exchanging houses,' he added.

Ellen nodded.

'I don't actually know him, but I've seen him around.'

'He lost his wife years ago and the house is too big for him. He might be pleased to move into a smaller house, especially one as well kept as yours.'

Ellen smiled a little at the praise. 'It's worth a try,' she said

The next day was Friday, and as usual, the queue at Jackie Miller's fish cart behind Trinity church and Doggart's shop on the High Street seemed to be a mile long. Ellen saw the old man a few places ahead of her and watched as he bought two kippers. Jackie wrapped them in newspaper; the old man paid for them and shuffled away.

'Poor soul,' the woman behind Ellen said. 'He's failing isn't he? They say his relatives are trying to put him in Fountains View. You wouldn't do that to a dog would you?'

'Indeed you wouldn't; they must have no shame,' a woman chimed in from further down the queue. 'Fountains View? What fountains? And those yellow bricks! They've changed the name but it still looks like the Workhouse, and it's still the same inside. Dormitories! All you get is a bed, a chair, and a locker.'

'Is he Mr Pattinson?' Ellen asked. 'And does he live on Bewick Road?

'That's right,' the woman behind her said. 'It's a lovely big house, but it's gone back a lot since his wife died. Like him, really,' she added. 'It's pitiful; they say he's not been right in the head since he lost her.'

Ellen collected her fish, put her basket on her arm and set off to walk home. Then she changed her mind and took the tramcar up to Bewick Road. 'Number 7', Mr Reid had said. She found the house. He might still be out, she thought, but she knocked at the door anyway and waited. Eventually Mr Pattinson answered. When she told him that the landlord, Mr Reid, had sent her, the old man became agitated.

'Is there something wrong? I've paid the rent! I'm sure I've paid the rent!'

'Of course you have. I haven't come about the rent. Mr Reid sent me because I'm looking for an exchange and he thought you might be interested.'

'An exchange? I don't know what you mean, pet.'

'He thought you might like to move to my house. It's much smaller; it would be easier for you to manage, and the rent is less than you pay here.'

'You mean leave me house?'

Ellen nodded.

'Oh no, pet, I couldn't do that. This is where me wife lived. I couldn't leave here, not for anything.'

Ellen could see behind him into the hallway; the floor was bare boards and the walls seemed to have a coat of very old distemper. It wasn't clean. But it was a big house. She took a deep breath and tried another tack.

An hour later, sitting in the kitchen in front of a miserable ash–blocked fire, she made her final offer.

'And I wouldn't have to cook?' the old man said.

'No, nor clean, or do shopping; and your washing and ironing would be done for you. You'd be treated like one of the family.'

'The family,' he repeated. 'You've got bairns?'

'Yes,' Ellen said patiently. 'That's why I need a bigger house.'

'We never had bairns; we'd have liked them,' he shook his head.

'So are we agreed?' Ellen asked gently. 'I can tell Mr Reid what we've arranged?'

'Aye, pet,' he nodded. 'It sounds alright to me. An' you can call me old John. Everybody calls me old John.'

'Are you sure about this, Ellen? Mr Reid asked. 'It wasn't exactly what I had in mind when I suggested an exchange.'

'But I can do it, can't I? Mr Pattinson will have his own room, and he'll be treated exactly the same as the rest of the family, and my name will go on the rent book. So no matter what happens it will be my house. I mean, you have no objections have you?'

'No, none at all, if that's what you want. But you'll be paying the rent, he'll have everything for nothing and there'll be a lot of extra work for you.'

'Washing, cooking and cleaning have to be done; one more won't make much difference,' she assured him. 'And there's all that space.'

'I can see you're set on it and you've made plans already,' Mr Reid said.

'I am and I have,' she agreed.

'Then I'd better give you the new rent book.'

Ellen wasted no time before going to Anderson and Garland's sale rooms and finding what she needed to make the house into a comfortable home: stair-carpet, rugs, extra furniture, crockery, table linen and ornaments all arrived in due course. She systematically scrubbed, cleaned and painted the house from top to bottom. When it was finished she hired Robsons the local haulage firm to move everything from the old house to the new one.

'Martha's coming to see me this afternoon,' old John announced one morning at breakfast time.

'Is she? That'll be nice for you,' Ellen said.

'That porridge was good,' he said, putting his spoon down and pushing the empty plate away. 'I haven't been bothered by her much up to now, have I?'

'You haven't,' Ellen agreed. 'Martha's your niece isn't she?'

'Aye, she is.' He got up from the table and picked up his tin box. It was a battered red and black cashbox with a chain and small padlock on it. He kept it with him: next to his plate on the table, on the chair by his bed at night, on his knee when he sat by the fire, and carried in a canvas satchel with the strap crossed over his chest, when he went out.

'She's my only living relative,' he said ponderously, 'me sister's lass. She heard I was ill.'

'Does she know you're better?' Ellen asked.

'Mebbe she does; I'm not sure.'

Martha arrived, and cast a dubious eye over the kitchen where old John liked to sit by the fire, but ran her hand appreciatively over the green chenille table cover before taking him away to the privacy of his own room.

'Family business,' she said crisply to Ellen.

They emerged a good half hour later.

Ellen offered the visitor some tea and they sat together stiffly in the front room. The blazing fire in the rarely-used grate hardly thawed the chill. Martha put her shiny leather handbag on the floor next to her shiny leather shoes. Old John held his tin box securely in his lap.

Martha eyes flicked around the room and came to rest on the ornamental dogs on the mantelpiece.

'They're rather attractive; Royal Worcester aren't they?'

'Staffordshire,' Ellen said quietly.

'I collect china and porcelain you know.'

Ellen said nothing but offered her a biscuit, which she refused.

'Never eat them, won't have them in the house – they play havoc with the waistline, don't they? I like the stair-carpet, Uncle; very nice. Axminster is it?'

'Ee, I wouldn't know, pet.'

'Now, the thing is,' she began, 'Uncle's getting no younger. And I know that he's not the brightest at the best of times, but this last illness has obviously affected him.'

'You knew he was ill, then?' she asked.

'I heard it on the High Street. I do think you might have informed me.'

'I don't know where you live.'

'Really? We live next to Saltwell Park. White-painted terrace; top of the street; very smart. My husband's a manager at Clarke Chapmans you know.'

'That's where she met him,' old John said sagely, 'she worked...'

'That's old news, Uncle,' Martha interrupted. 'Let's not be boring. As I was saying, I think you should have informed me. Anyway, no matter; there's no harm done. Uncle's obviously much better now. But it was a shock; we might have lost him.' She looked at her uncle with concern and patted his knee. He moved his tin box out of her reach. 'You've done your best for Uncle, and I'm grateful, but I feel he should spend his declining years with his family.'

'I understand that,' Ellen replied. 'Family's good.'

'Aye; but I'm not too sure meself,' the old man objected.

'Oh Uncle,' Martha said tartly, 'let's not go through this again. You know you'll be better off with me. I've got a big house by the park and a garden you can sit in.'

'Aye, I know that, but I'm used to this house, and Ellen.'

'Well, have it your own way. I'm not going to argue with you, but never say I didn't offer.' Martha handed Ellen her china cup and saucer and stood up. She picked up her bag with one hand and quickly brushed down the front of her skirt with the other, then gave the hem of her jacket a sharp tug. 'I'll see myself out,' she said, turning on her heel and leaving the room.

'She was always bossy,' old John said, 'and that was before she went to work at Clarkies and met her man.'

'Was she a secretary or a typist?' Ellen asked.

'Why no, pet, she was never in an office, she worked in the canteen. She was a skivvy, although you'd never know it to look at her these days. And now I've upset her.'

'Don't worry,' Ellen reassured him, 'she'll be back.'

And she was; the next weekend, and the next, and a few more after that.

Finally the old man capitulated. He collected his few belongings, and a beige Slater's taxi came all the way from Newcastle Central Station to drive him to the white-fronted house by the park. He carried his tin box himself.

A couple of days later Martha called; she wanted to know why so few of Uncle's possessions had been sent with him. She had come to collect them.

'He took all his things with him,' Ellen told her.

'But what about glassware, and rugs, and ornaments? Why, for instance, didn't he bring the Staffordshire dogs? And what about the Westminster chimes clock?'

'He didn't bring them because they aren't his; I have the receipts if you want to see them. This is my house; your uncle was living with us, not the other way round. And you specifically said that you didn't want any of the things from his room. They're still there if you've changed your mind.'

'I wouldn't have ...stuff...like that in my house,' Martha retorted with a shudder.

'Well, that's all he had,' Ellen said.

Over the next few months Ellen heard snippets about old John. It seemed that his return to the bosom of his family was turning out to be a little less than idyllic. Then in the winter, she heard that he was ill. The week after Christmas she heard that he'd died.

She went to the funeral in the cemetery below the park. It was a pitiful affair on a bitterly cold day; a handful of mourners stood by the graveside in flurries of snow. A single wreath of small white chrysanthemums and Ellen's bunch of blue and yellow forced irises were the only flowers lying on the grass waiting to be placed on the grave's fresh soil.

Martha was dressed in black from head to toe and kept dabbing her eyes with her lace-edged handkerchief. When the first handful of earth was sprinkled on to the coffin lid she seemed close to collapse.

Afterwards, she thanked Ellen for coming.

'We're devastated,' she said. 'I'd invite you back, but you'll appreciate that this is a time for his family, the reading of the will and so on...'

'Your uncle John left a will?' Ellen said, surprised.

'Oh yes, it's to be read after the funeral. Fothergill and Fothergill on Grey Street did everything for us – I mean – for him. Poor dear Uncle,' she put on a brave smile, 'he did have his little ways didn't he? He was most insistent that his affairs should be properly ordered. For the family, you understand. But I must go now...'

'Of course,' Ellen said. 'The family.'

Next morning there was an imperious knock on Ellen's front door. When she opened it Martha was standing there, breathless, patches of heightened colour in her cheeks, and her mouth as tight as a zip. She was still in blackest black from head to foot but her hat was askew. She barged past Ellen.

'Do come in,' Ellen murmured as she closed the door.

She found Martha standing with her back to the kitchen fire, clutching a brown paper bag in her black suede-gloved hands. She glared at Ellen, took a step nearer to the table and plonked the bag down.

'How do you explain this?' she demanded, pointing a shaking finger at the bag.

'I don't know. What is it?' Ellen asked.

'Look inside!'

Ellen looked; it was old John's tin box, minus its padlock and chain.

'Take it out!' Martha hissed.

Ellen took it out of the bag and placed it on the table.

'Open it! No, I'll do it for you!' Martha snatched the box, but couldn't prise it open with her gloved fingers.

Ellen took the box from her without a word, lifted the catch and opened it.

'You see what's in it?'

'Yes,' Ellen said quietly, putting it back on the table.

'My goodness you must have seen me coming! You had all his money, and then when he needed looking after, you sent him to me! He cost a fortune to keep: the extra heating, lighting, hot water for baths; and he ate us out of house and home.' Martha's voice was rising on every syllable. 'We even paid for his will, and his funeral and he left us... THAT!' She jabbed the tin box with her finger.

'It must be upsetting,' Ellen said.

'Upsetting? Upsetting doesn't begin to cover it! Don't tell me you didn't know. It's false pretences! I' m going to take you to court!'

'It'll be the rock you perish on if you do! You'll be wasting your time; I don't know whether your uncle ever had any money, he lived here rent free. And if I remember rightly, you were the one who persuaded him to come to you. Your uncle's estate is not my concern.'

'Estate! Hah! That's a joke! This is ALL he left! And he had the ...the cheek...to give it to the solicitor to keep for him! We had to pay an extra fee for it! No wonder he wanted the will read *after* the funeral! Had I known, I wouldn't have...'

'Buried him?' Ellen finished for her.

'Would you? Would anybody? Look at it! Stuffed full of...' Martha picked the box up and banged it on the table. 'STRING! Bits of string! LITTLE bits of string!' her voice broke. 'They're too short even to tie together to make one long piece!'

Ellen could feel the smile twitching the side of her mouth.

'Well, I'm sorry for your disappointment,' she said, 'especially if you thought it was full of banknotes, or insurance policies; but it's nothing to do with me. And I'd like you to go now. I'll see you out.'

Martha stared at her.

'Here,' Ellen said, scooping the bits of string and the cash box back into the paper bag. 'Don't go without your tin box.'

Martha took it.

Ellen followed her as she walked unsteadily along the passage, then closed the front door behind her. She leaned against it.

'And they said old John was daft,' she laughed.

Goebbel's House

Pauline Plummer

When I saw the Wall being pulled apart on the TV news, I thought about Berlin for the first time in years. I thought of the faces of people who had once been dear to me and I thought of my father who found it difficult to forgive.

We took the tram on a hot day. I was sweating through my British Home Stores blouse and slacks and I was sure that Dieter could feel my sweating palm in his hand. We boarded the S Bahn at Zoologisches Garten. Through the smeared windows I saw Kurfurstendam and the huge Prussian buildings of the city gradually merge into suburban wooden houses and gardens bursting with soft fruit.

Our long legs flew like lances through the forest of pine, birch and oak beyond Wannsee Station, two tall teenagers with rucksacks and a small tent, one dark brown head and one red head – young, handsome and healthy.

It was cool under the trees even though the leaves were crisped, burnt from the intense heat of late summer. I was a Northern English girl and not used to Eastern European weather – windless and sultry with the air hundreds of miles from a wash of sea. We stood still to listen to the drum tap of woodpeckers and then marched on, crunching fallen cones on a carpet of leaves.

We heard the shouts and laughter of swimmers in the lake before we saw it. It cost money to enter the fenced-off swimming area – there was an iron turnstile – and we had both just finished school and had no money.

'I have camped to this lake many times. Through the trees we can find other beach type place to swim.' Dieter spoke in his thick German accent which I no longer noticed. I used to think of war films but it had become so dear to me I didn't hear the harsh consonants and flat vowels.

We crossed the curved stone bridge onto Schwannen-werder Island, lush with olive leaved trees in the overgrown gardens of abandoned mansions. Wooden shutters hung off the windows at awkward angles. A pigeon flew out of a smashed window as we walked past. Weeds and wildflowers bent in the deeply shadowed eaves and passageways.

We found a curve of shingle and reeds. I turned my back and stripped off my blouse and slacks – to my swimsuit underneath. It felt intimate this undressing under the shade of a willow and I tugged at the bottom of my swimsuit. We held hands and walked into the cold water and although the hot sun burned my white and freckled shoulders I shivered. As we swam away from the bank, the water turned from blue to brown, suddenly deepening.

We trod water and Dieter pulled me to wrap me in darkly tanned arms. I could see my legs moving like large fish through the stippled water.

'You are white, like a swan Eileen,' he said.

Only a few miles away were wooden turrets with guards

holding machine guns. The border was mined and there were stories of people being blown up as they tried to escape to the West. The world was on a constant state of nuclear alert but we dissolved in one wet, river-drenched kiss in blazing sun at three in the afternoon.

We lay on our washed and washed again towels under the shade of a willow. He rested his head on one arm and looked down at me tracing the shape of my ginger brown eyebrows with his finger.

'You don't know what this island is, do you Eileen?'

'Is it something special?'

'This is where the top Nazis lived during the war. Those houses.'

'Is that why they're abandoned?'

'Well. Yes. We could sleep in one. That one over there is Goebbels' villa. I have been inside. Then we don't have to erect tent, not true?'

'Goebbels!'

'Yes, it is fine house. Not too much rubbish. We can be alone in room Eileen. Do you want that? To be with me?'

I knew all about the graded levels of sin from my religious lessons but how much I enjoyed this press of body on body. I let him touch and kiss my breasts but not beneath my swimsuit. And as he was a good boy, he didn't want to do what was not pleasing to me. As I lay beneath the willow I knew I would remember this day. I didn't know what would happen but I hungered for something.

'We could zip the sleeping bags together.' This was the most I was going to admit to. We had spent almost all the waking hours of this exchange together. His parents in their wooden house welcomed me and filled me up with German delicacies so that my willowy body was curving outwards. I did not wonder about their lives. I did not ask what Dieter's father did in the war, or his mother. I had just taken my A-levels so my head was full of the couplets of Catullus, obscure, irregular French verbs and *The Waste Land*. The war was something that happened to my father but about which he never talked. As Dieter and his family didn't talk. Except for the Russians. Dieter's mother had talked about the Russians taking Berlin and started to weep.

The main door of blistered wood and paint hung on its hinges. There was a wrecked doll in the passageway, its clothes torn and dirty, and a few wooden bricks. Did they belong to Goebbels' children? Nazi children. Wood pigeons coo-cooed in the garden and the heavy branches of a willow rustled. Our own voices echoed in the dark hallway.

We could smell the must and damp of rooms that hadn't been lived in for decades. I could smell my own sweat and Dieter's male smell mixed with lake water. There was a crooked and cracked mirror on the wall. We looked like two swans gliding along a lake. My white blouse stuck to me now. I gripped his hand, this masculine hand with dark hairs on the back and lower joints of the fingers, but he pulled away.

'I will go and find a room that is not dirty where we put our sleeping bags. Wait here.'

I kicked some litter out of the way and noticed old sheets of newspaper dated 1962, five years ago, with a photograph of

President Kennedy on the front.

'Whose is all this stuff? We shouldn't be here. This is an evil place.'

'Don't you trust me? This is only time we can spend the night together, alone.'

He opened the door into a room and closed it behind us. We lowered our backpacks. He put his arm around me and began to unbutton my blouse, pulling out a breast from its cotton cup and kissing it. I looked down at his short dark hair and the shape of his head bent over. It was dusk. A soft pink light floated through the windows and the sun was setting over the lake. We put down our sleeping bags on the dusty wooden floor. There was still an old key in the lock so Dieter turned it.

It was quiet. The wood pigeons in the garden: water lapping against a bank. I lit a candle. The flame cast our elongated shadows against the wall as we slipped into the sleeping bag. Dieter's hands became more daring. I began to tremble. I felt like a wild animal caught in a net. These were my secret places.

That was when we heard the footstep. And another footstep moving along the hallway outside. We stopped and looked at each other and lay still without a word, not knowing what to do, not knowing who was out there. The footsteps were close to the door. We saw the door handle being turned. Then, who or whatever was out there became angry and shook the door, but Dieter had locked it with an enormous rusting key.

My heart beat so fast I thought whoever was there must

hear it. Dieter got out of the sleeping bag and stood still, legs apart. I reached for the candle and blew it out though my hand shook so much, the hot wax spilled on my skin and on the floor. Through the window we could see the moon had risen.

The door was shaken again and we stiffened. I knew that Dieter did not know what to do. We had nothing with us to defend ourselves from whoever was out there. Was the intruder human or spirit? Did it mean us harm or was it a tramp, perhaps left over from the war, who lived here? We did not say these things to each other. I made the sign of the cross and said the rosary silently on my fingers, even while thinking that I was about to sin - so who would listen to me?

There was a long intense waiting while we stayed rigid and silent. The door was tried one last time and then footsteps.

'Perhaps he will wait for us to come out the room,' Dieter whispered. 'Then he may attack us. Safer to stay inside.'

I nodded but my mouth could make no words. We heard a door banging far away and a motorboat on the lake but then outside we heard footsteps on the gravel.

It occurred to me that he might have looked in on us when the candle was burning. What did he want? I knew there were sadistic men. I knew how the SS had tortured people. I knew about concentration camps and gas chambers. Where was Dieter's father during the war?

'Don't be afraid Eileen. I will take care of you.'

Even in the moonlight I could see how soft his brown eyes were. He stroked my hair. We were both kids, trying on love for size for the first time. How could this tall skinny eighteen year old defend us from some larger older man who might have had a gun left from the war? But I knew he would not run away and save himself. He must have been exhausted with the effort of appearing calm and brave so he lay down beside my trembling body.

As the moon travelled its way through the sky the moonlit shadows changed angles. We waited and waited for dawn. Perhaps one of us fitfully fell asleep. Gradually the room began to fill with grey light. A blackbird sang its passionate song in the garden. Strangely I wondered whether Mutti would have made us more plum cake last night. And then I thought of the border guards up in their turrets turning to face over the wall into the West. The light became rosier and warmer. I knew that we would be able to leave the room soon. I wondered where the intruder was now. Was he hiding in undergrowth in the woods? Was there a cellar, a bunker left from the War?

As soon as the sky became blue, Dieter unlocked the door ever so quietly and holding hands we ran with all of our youth out through this hallway and out through the broken door and along the road onto the bridge back to home singing and shouting.

BIOGRAPHICAL NOTES

Amanda Baker is best known in the North East for her unique character-based sketch-style comedy performance poetry. She has performed at the Edinburgh Fringe 2010/11/12. In 2011 one of her poems was short listed in the Bridport International Poetry Prize and one of her comedy pieces appears in *The Iron Anthology of New Humorous Verse*. Under pseudonym Adnam Arekab she has published *Chronicles of Eleanor Catherine – Long Limbed Green Eyed Dragon Slayer*. The third book *Eleanor & the Dragon Runt* is now available on Amazon in hard copy and as an e-book. Amanda runs a weekly blog *<http://browngirlsoutsidethering.blogspot.co.uk/>*.

Rosemary Brydon was born and bred on Tyneside, but lived for thirty years in North Yorkshire. She came home seven years ago. She was a teacher in the North East and in Yorkshire. She was a local correspondent for three Yorkshire newspapers, and a regular columnist for both the *Gazette* and *Herald*, and the Anglican Archdiocesan paper *SEEN*. With her husband she edited the Middlesbrough RC paper *The Catholic Voice*.

Fiona Cooper is the author of ten novels, including *Rotary Spokes* and *As You Desire Me*. Her work has been described as iconoclastic, wildly funny and on the edge. She was involved in the Orange short story competition and judges the monthly Global Short Story competition. Fiona does writing, spiritual workshops, regression therapy and personal literary tutoring and critiques. Having survived the Thatcher cull, she escaped to a field in the North East and plans one day to live in a tree. She is involved in all aspects of spiritual exploration and cosmic energy and hopes that some day it will all make sense.

Crista Ermiya was born and grew up in London, of Filipino and Turkish-Cypriot parentage. She moved to the North East in 2002 where she is a freelance writer and editor, and works on the interdisciplinary academic journal *Landscape Research* at Newcastle University. She is married with one son. Crista won the Decibel Penguin Short Story Prize with her story *Maganda* (published in *New Voices From A Diverse Culture*, Penguin 2007). A book of short stories is due out in Autumn 2013 (Red Squirrel Press).

Beda Higgins has stories and poetry published in a selection of anthologies and collections, including being the first prize winner of the *Mslexia* short story competition 2009. Her first collection of short stories *Chameleon* was published by IRON Press in 2011. *Chameleon* was chosen as a Read Regional Recommendation and was on the Long-list for the Edge Hill Short Story Prize 2012. In 2010 she received a Time to Write Award for her third novel. She is a regular contributor to *Independent Nurse Journal* (writing as Bernadette Higgins). She is married with three children and lives in Newcastle upon Tyne. <www.bedahiggins.org>

Eileen Jones lives in Tynedale and is the editor of *The IRON Book of New Humorous Verse*. A pamphlet of her own poetry is due in October 2013 from Red Squirrel Press and a full collection of poems, *The Pale Handbag of the Apocalypse* is due from IRON Press in 2014. Her play *Knives* was produced by New Writing North in 2006.

Avril Joy was born and brought up on the Somerset Levels, the setting for her novel *The Sweet Track*, published in 2007 by Flambard Press. She now lives and works in the North East of England, near Bishop Auckland. Her most recent novel, *Blood Tide*, is a crime novel set in Newcastle and Weardale. In this new venture into crime fiction she draws on her long experience of life inside a women's prison, having worked for a number of years as a teacher, and subsequently as Head of Learning and Skills, at HMP Low Newton, Durham City. In 2012 she was shortlisted for The Bristol Prize and she won the inaugural Costa Short Story Award, 2013. She blogs regularly at <www.avriljoy.com>

Pauline Plummer is a poet and short story writer who has lived in the North East since 1982, though originally from Liverpool. Her most recent poetry collection is *Bint* (Red Squirrel Press); her verse novella *From Here to Timbuktu* (Smokestack Press) has been chosen as a Read Regional book by New Writing North. IRON Press published her poetry collection, *Demon Straightening* in 1999. She teaches creative writing at Northumbria University and the Open University as well as in community projects in UK and abroad.

John N Price lives in Washington and was born in South Shields. He was a teacher for most of his career before running a successful TVEI project at the *Sunderland Echo*. He is married with two children. He has had a children's novel (*Beasts of Plenty* – Macmillan) published under the pen name John Kirkham and a darkly comic novel (*Suicide City* – Wild Wolf) published under the pen name Jake Pattison. He has won prizes for short stories (Gateshead Libraries) and poetry (*The Journal*). Now retired, he writes for fun.

Angela Readman is a winner of the National Flash Fiction Day Competition, *Inkspill* magazine short story competition, and the runner up of The Short Story Competition 2011. Her stories have recently been shortlisted in the Asham Short Story Prize and the Bristol Short Story Prize. She was one of the new poets in the IRON Press collection *Unholy Trinity* (2002).

Jane Roberts-Morpeth lives on the North East coast where she is frequently to be found wandering the streets on a quest for sea monsters and the perfect cappuccino. A self-confessed nerd, fantasy and sci-fi devotee, she graduated from Northumbria University with an MA in Creative Writing. *Charybdis* won Story Tyne 2011 and is her first publication. Jane is currently completing her first novel, an urban fantasy set in Northumberland concerning disaffected youth and the perfidy of angels.

Shelley Day Sclater was born in Newcastle and educated at Edinburgh and Cambridge Universities. She has been a lawyer, an academic psychologist and a research professor. *Picnicking with my Father* won the 2010 Lit & Phil Ghost Story Competition, was commended in the Aesthetica Creative Works Competition in the same year, and was published in *The Journal* in 2012. She earns a crust by freelancing. In 2011 her first novel *The Confession of Stella Moon* was shortlisted for the UEA Charles Pick Fellowship, and went on to win New Writing North's Andrea Badenoch Award. Shelley is currently working on a novel for children set in Northumberland, and a collection of short stories.

Stephen Shieber was born in Germany in 1975. He lives in Newcastle upon Tyne and is a graduate of Northumbria University's Creative Writing MA. His short fiction has appeared in various places online, as well as in both print and e-book anthologies. His first collection of stories, *Being Normal*, was published by Tonto Books in 2008. Stephen is currently completing a novel called *A Very Queer Cure* as well as a new collection of short stories and micro-fictions, titled *Leaving the Room with Dignity*.

Judy Walker lives in Northumberland and attends a weekly writing group in Newcastle, from which she gains huge inspiration. She has an MA in Creative Writing from Newcastle University and won the UKA Opening Pages Award in 2007 for her first children's novel *Frankie*, which was published by UKA Press in November 2008. Her short stories have been published in anthologies and magazines (including *Mslexia*) and broadcast on BBC Radio. Her drama work has been performed in Northumberland, Tyne & Wear and London. She is currently working on a novel set in Northern Ireland during the Troubles. When she's not writing Judy loves to bake cakes and collect eaves-droppings.

Rob Walton has performed, written and taught in the North East for a number of years. He has written gardening columns for the *Hull Daily Mail*, an online schools' resource for the Tyneside Cinema, columns for Scunthorpe United's matchday programme, books for teachers and numerous articles for education magazines. In 2012 he worked with sculptor Russ Coleman and the local community to write the text for the New Hartley Memorial Pathway. His short stories *Lenny Bolton Changes Trains* and *The Yellow Tulips* were recently published in *Stations* by Arachne Press. He lives in North Shields with his family.